Are You Satisfied Yet?

by

MBridges

Katrina
Peace : Blessings
—M[illegible]
5/2008

Are you satisfied, yet?

Are you satisfied, yet? is a work of fiction. Any resemblance to actual persons and/or events is strictly coincidental. References to actual places and/or historic events are meant to enhance the story and provide a realistic setting for the novel.

For information regarding permission to make copies of any part of the work please visit:
www.lofpublishing.com

ISBN: 0-9764441-0-0
ISBN: 978-0-9764441-0

Cover Design by: N'Digodesign.com
Interior by: LOF Publishing
Houston, Texas
Edited by: Kathleen Marusak

Printed in the United States of America

Are you satisfied, yet?

LOF Publishing

Acknowledgements

My intentions were to write a word of thanks to everyone who helped turn my dream into a reality, but the list kept going on and on. When I could see that it was getting too long, I'd edit it, but then feel bad that someone had to be deleted. I'd hope they'd understand that their help was valuable to me as well and it was all a matter of available space. I've decided to condense my list and make certain that I get everyone by simply saying, "Thank you. I could not have done this alone...I *did not* do this alone."

Other Titles to watch for:

Too Deep For Tears

Getting up and Getting on

This story is dedicated to all my readers. Thanks for being the audience I've always craved...

One

Have you ever felt like there was just too much weight on your heart? That the strain of taking another breath would be too great and the effort alone would kill you? Yeah, well that's how Betty Jean felt every day of her life. Every day that she opened her eyes and saw another one of the Lord's glorious mornings, she felt betrayed. Each night she went to bed, she said her prayers, always making a special point of asking forgiveness for her sins. In case the Lord answered her prayers and she woke to this world no more, she would be ready.

Betty Jean was simply tired, that's all. It wasn't so much that she was tired of life. She was just tired of her life. The day to day bullshit she had to deal with. She was educated. She held two Masters Degrees, Finance and Accounting. She had a great job as a financial analyst that she loved. She lived in a two-story, three bedroom house and drove a fully loaded midnight blue Infiniti Q45 with peanut butter interior.

She had everything that most little girls who wanted to be the shit when they grew up, dreamed of having.

Including her man.

Ezekiel Johnson.

One smooth ass brother, fine as hell, and he knew how to make paper, not just spend someone else's. He and Betty Jean met six years ago at a Black Arts Fund Raiser. Ezekiel was a good man, but he had one big problem that always managed to become Betty Jean's problem. He was a player. Tried and true to the game. It was impossible for him to be faithful. No matter how much he professed to love her, their relationship was only monogamous when he was between women.

Betty Jean may have had what little girls wanted, but she was a grown woman. Full grown and she was tired of playing games. Unfortunately, Ezekiel Johnson was a master at the sport and from where she stood; there wasn't an end in sight. This was passing tragic, because Betty Jean didn't want to play anymore. What she wanted to do was pick up her shovel and bucket, leave the sandbox and tell the rest of the children to kiss her ass.

She felt that way even now as she snuggled deeper into Ezekiel's arms, like she never wanted to leave. And way deep down inside, somewhere, she still felt that way. But closer to the surface, where her hurts were not buried so deep, she wanted to flee his touch. She wanted to take her toys and run home, but even in the unconscious state of sleep, he would not release her.

He held her gently; securely anchoring her to him by cupping her left breast in his sleeping hand. His body spooned to hers, as it had for six years. Lying as they were, she could smell his cologne. She inhaled, closing her eyes.

Liz for Men

It was his habit to wear Liz on what Betty Jean liked to call "date night." Carla, she supposed, liked Liz, but then, so did Betty Jean. In fact, it was her regard for the fragrance that made her buy it for him. Now he hardly ever wore it, unless it was date night. Date night was not hers. She'd only get a whiff of it as he left out the door to live his lie, or like now, when he returned home, but it was a rarity for him to wear it for her benefit.

She sighed heavily, willing her heart to stop beating. It hurt too much. She squeezed her eyes shut and held her breath, waiting. Nothing happened. She could still feel life stubbornly swirling around her.

Zeke moved against her until his groin cradled her backside; the back of her thighs pressed firmly to the front of his. She was practically in his lap. His contentment more complete, he sighed. She could feel his breath on the back of her neck and she tried not to let the warm pleasure of it arouse her. If she turned in his arms and moved against him the way he liked, soft and slow, he would have an excuse.

He who was never tired would be exhausted. The man, who made exquisite love to her once while burning with a one hundred and three degree temperature, would be felled by a headache or something he *ate at the club* would have him lying low, preventing him from making love to her that night. Not on date night. Never on date night. Date night was Carla's night to hold him.

But he'd be back in the saddle come morning. All ills forgotten. Miraculously cured in a matter of hours, he'd be ready to make up for the lost night. She assumed his conscience would let him have sex with another woman just not on the same night as with her, but apparently he had no such restrictions the next morning. His sins were washed away and he was born again with the coming of the dawn, she supposed. Ezekiel only made up his tired little excuses because he didn't know she knew about Carla.

But Betty Jean prided herself, well, as much pride as she had left, which wasn't much, on being an intelligent, black woman. It was that and the fact that she knew her man. He couldn't deceive her, unless she let him. She had to willingly go along with whatever bit of ridiculousness he was telling her, in order for her to be deceived. It didn't just happen. She didn't find out about shit he did years later. She was as aware of his lies and deceit as he was. She just didn't say anything to him about what she knew.

Betty Jean knew him too well for a lie to go undetected. She knew where his skeletons were hidden; where all the bodies were buried, so to speak. Yes, Betty Jean knew her man. Not one of those sugary *I Know Him So Well* kinds of knowledge, but one of those *A Lie Is About To Fall Out His Mouth* types and damned if you aren't holding a bone two seconds later. Yet, another skeleton revealed! Another fucking lie. Exactly. Now that was the way that Betty Jean knew Ezekiel Johnson. She could see the lie forming on his lips before he even finished speaking it.

And she saw the blasphemy of Carla long ago. Saw it in his face, lurking in his eyes. Felt it in his touch. Even before she'd found proof.

That's why she was still awake at 4:22 in the morning. That's why she felt like her heart was too heavy to breathe. Because she knew her man. She didn't have to guess or wonder. She *knew* that just a few hours before, the body that was currently molded firmly to hers was folding into someone else's. Those exquisite hands of his were sliding across some other woman's breasts.

He had carelessly taken from another what she would have freely given him. He would have gotten more from the experience, too, in her mind. With Carla, all they could possibly have was sex. When their bodies came together, that's all there was, a joining of flesh. But when Ezekiel loved Betty Jean he held more than just her body. He held her heart, her soul in his grasp. Tonight would have been no different. When Betty Jean made love to Ezekiel, the joining melded her spirit to his and they were one. She liked watching his face when he loved her. The play of expressions and emotions were always her undoing. But tonight another had watched that face.

Now Betty Jean lay hurting, trying not to breathe because it was too painful. The simple action threatened tears. Betty Jean closed her eyes, seeking sleep once again. Ezekiel would want breakfast in the morning. She usually ate on the go, a soda and a donut her only nourishment, but he preferred something from home. She once loved frying his eggs and bacon. The simple act made her feel like she was taking care of him. Now someone else was taking care of him. Thinking of Ezekiel caused her to inhale. She filled herself with his scent, if not his body. She sighed heavily again, wishing that morning would pass her over.

For the hundredth time that night, she wondered what was so great about Carla.

**

Four hours later, in a small apartment on the southeast side of town, Carla Jeffries was wondering nearly the same thing. What was so fucking great about being Carla? This morning, especially, she sure as hell didn't know.

She pulled heavily on the cigarillo blunt that hung between her cherry cola red lips and said patiently into the phone, for what felt like the millionth time, "Look, I already told you, Eric, I can't get to work before ten o'clock. I don't have a car and I'm not riding the bus that damned early in the morning to get way the hell over there, just because that jackass keeps putting me on the schedule for six and seven o'clock."

She listened to the irate voice of her shift manager on the other end of the line and rolled her eyes towards the ceiling. "This is such shit, Eric, and you know it. He's mad because his dumb ass finally figured out he won't ever get any pussy from me, so he's screwing around with my goddamned money. My fucking livelihood. And instead of you telling him to grow up, deal with the shit and press on like a good little soldier, you decide to suspend me for three days. Isn't that some shit, Eric? Especially knowing I'm about to hang up the fucking phone and call me a lawyer."

"Momma?" a tiny voice called to her, accompanied by a tiny hand that patted her leg.

Carla covered the phone with her hand. "I'm on the phone, sweet pea, go tell your daddy what you want, okay?" Smiling, she watched the little girl walk away to locate her father. "Yeah, I'm still here," she paused, listening. "I can be there at ten or maybe eleven, since it's already so late." She tapped ashes from her blunt into the kitchen trash can. "I still need to leave by whatever time the schedule has on it, Eric. Not my problem. Talk to your boy about that, he shouldn't have put me on the schedule for seven to three."

She listened further, shaking her head in the negative. "No. No, Eric. Stop letting your boy screw me over. Either I leave at three or I'm not coming in at all."

She spoke for a few more seconds before ending the conversation. She hung up the phone, mumbling and cursing. Thomas entered the kitchen. Walking up behind her, he put his arms around her slender waist. He bent and kissed her neck. "Hey, baby."

She pulled deeply on the small cigar once again. Turning in his arms, she blew the smoke into his face. Thomas frowned and waved it away, releasing her. Carla crossed the kitchen to pull the refrigerator door open. Displaying its frugal contents, she asked, "Can *my* baby eat tonight?" referring to the little girl who'd just left the kitchen.

Thomas looked from Carla to the refrigerator and back. His lengthy appraisal caused Carla to raise one dark brow in challenge. A menacing look of her own was written across her face. Today she wore a wig of deep burgundy that hung to the middle of her back. The bangs fell long in her face. They brushed her eyebrows, just barely kissing her lashes. She tossed her head, flipping the bangs from her eyes. She wanted Thomas to have an unobstructed view of her face. She didn't have time for any fucking misunderstandings this morning. She wanted him to read it in her eyes that she wasn't down for no bullshit. *Too damned early in the morning,* she thought. Thomas had raised his hand against her once and she was sure as certain he would not do it again, but every now and then he really looked like he was thinking about it. Something she couldn't fathom would darken his gaze and she was sure he was thinking about putting his hands on her.

But striking her again would always be only something that crossed his mind. She'd surprised him, that was for damned sure, but really he shouldn't have been surprised. As long as she and Thomas had been together, knowing Carla as he did, he should have known that she would not take an ass beating meekly, willingly.

Not again.

But she had.

She let him vent his anger without comment or reproach. She suffered a slap or two, a bruised shoulder from where she hit the wall and a bottom lip she'd nearly bitten through. Afterwards, he apologized. He had not meant to lose control like that. Especially not against his Carla. He never wanted to hurt her, he'd said and he cried. It was the second time she'd seen Thomas shed tears. The first time was when he held their baby girl right after she was born. And then the tears that coursed through his apology and chased after it. Even through the blinding fog of her hurt and disbelief, Carla could tell that the tears were different.

When he held Ebony, he cried because she was so beautiful and he loved her and she was his. Words could not have done his happiness justice, so he simply held her and wept. Carla remembered the sight of his tears that night, and how they had made her love him more, but the tears of his apology were met with a cold heart. They touched no part of her. She knew why he cried that time, as well; he cried because he'd hurt her. He loved her and he hurt her and she was his. His to love and protect from harm. His to keep safe. And he had failed.

While he apologized, Carla hadn't said a word. She waited quietly for him to stop speaking, then went into the bathroom to wipe her face. She noticed in the mirror over the sink that the blood from her lip had dripped onto her favorite shirt. A midriff light blue tee that tied in a knot at the back and had *Sassy* splashed across the front.

She pulled the shirt over her head, wincing at the pain in her left shoulder. She could see the beginnings of a dark bruise forming, compliments of the wall she'd hit. The side of her face had a slight glow from where she'd been slapped. Tentatively, she worked her jaw in the mirror, but it felt okay. It was a little sore, but she wouldn't miss any meals because of it. Her lip hurt like a son of a bitch, but she'd live.

She turned off the bathroom light. When she returned to the adjoining bedroom she wore only her panties and socks. She'd sat on the edge of the bed rolling a joint. The turning motion hurt her lip, but she continued, watching the faint streaks of red taint the white of the paper. Her hands shook slightly.

Thomas was on the bed with his back to her. He'd lain on his side with his arm wrapped tightly around a pillow. He was only pretending to be asleep, though. She knew there was no goddamned way he could kick her ass like that, then just fall asleep. No goddamned way. She'd know he was full of shit even if she couldn't hear him sniffling quietly. His weak ass just didn't want to deal with what he'd done, so he sought an avenue of escape. He knew he couldn't talk to her. She wasn't listening and he was too goddamned scared to leave while she cooled off. He knew she'd never let him come back. Instead, he'd pretend to be asleep, until it actually grabbed hold of him.

It's okay, Carla told herself that night. *Let him pretend.* She slid to the floor, keeping her back against the side of the bed.

It was just past ten in the evening, if the clock on the night stand was to be believed. And she had no reason to doubt it; though, her small body ached like days had passed since Thomas's rage, instead of an hour.

Carla remembered sitting on the floor in her bedroom. She sat in the dark blowing smoke and listening. It was after midnight when she heard Thom's breathing even out in genuine slumber. Her mind had not relaxed as she had hoped. She reached under the bed retrieving her "supplies" box. Normally, she didn't need so much weed to free her mind; especially not this late at night, but tonight the world held her chained to it and she really needed to fly. She thought about Thom faking sleep when he wanted to escape the thoughts in his head. When she wanted to hide from herself she chose to hang out with old chums, Mary Jane being her companion of choice. MJ was her girl and was always on board for a toke. When her reality became too damn real to handle, Mary could always be counted upon to help her make a clean getaway.

She turned on the closet light, then sat on the floor to open the Nike shoe box. She removed a cigar and a thin razor from the shoe box. She held the razor in her hand. She turned it over, looking at it. It felt good clasped between her fingers. *Really* good. Too good. But she had no plans to cut Thom. Even if he did deserve it. She let the razor sink smoothly into the flavored cigar. With one hand she held it while dumping the exposed tobacco onto the lid of her shoe box. She used tiny sewing scissors to snip the top off the empty wrapper before licking it. She refilled the shell from a small plastic bag. Using her lighter, she dried the newly resealed crease.

She lit her creation, inhaling strongly, then she held the smoke for a long moment before releasing it through her nose. She pulled again, closing her eyes. Finally, she exhaled, letting the smoke circle her head like a silvery halo. She kept replaying the night in her head, reliving Thomas's brutality again and again. Thomas had actually struck her. Her Thomas. The father of her child had raised his hand against her. She still couldn't believe it. She had loved Thomas so hard, so strong, for so long, how could he? He knew what she'd lived through. How she'd grown up. His violence had not been deserved. She had never done anything to warrant such treatment. She had been true to Thom. He'd been the only man she'd ever known and he would beat her. He'd raise his hand to her over some bullshit he heard. A lie he was told.

She sat in the darkened room, hurting from both her head and her heart.

She blew smoke out through her nose, shaking her head slowly.

She sat staring at the clock, resting her tongue gently against her lip where it still throbbed slightly. It was past three-thirty in the morning before she rose from the floor to creep down the hall to her child's room. She went to the closet, sat on the floor in her Victoria's Secret underwear and pulled off her socks. Twisting the nose from her daughter's piggy bank, she'd let the coins fall into the thin cotton fabric.

When her socks were filled, she returned to her room. She walked over to the bed where Thomas lay. He had turned from his side onto his back and she was pleased by the show of consideration. She could not believe the amount of love she held for him. She gave him everything she had. Everything she was and he would strike her in anger. Jealous over her, who had always been true. She had been struck without just cause by a man who said he loved her.

It was not right.

The first blow, hitting him dead center chest, woke Thomas from his sleep. If he thought he was dreaming, the second strike that landed on his upper right thigh assured him it was no dream. And Carla's shouting, "You son-of-a-bitch!" with every blow she swung, cleared up any remaining doubts he may have had.

When she was finished her hands hurt from gripping the socks so tightly for so long. Thomas lay on the bed in a ball hurting like she had been. He had not fought back or tried to defend himself other than shielding his head. She guessed he knew he deserved it.

That night, she rented the movie *The Burning Bed.* They'd watched it together in near silence. At the end, when Farah Fawcett set the bed on fire ending her abusive husband's life, she looked pointedly at Thomas sitting quietly across from her on the couch. She had not said a word. She hadn't needed to. While he may have misjudged her the previous evening, he now understood what Carla would and would not tolerate with crystal clear clarity.

Absently, he rubbed his side where an ugly bruise had developed. Neither of them spoke of what she had done to him, but neither did they discuss what he'd done to cause it. But a new understanding had begun and their relationship was changed. Gone was the Carla that looked at him with love in her eyes and greeted him with a kiss on her lips. She was replaced with a sullen woman, filled with attitude, who didn't welcome Thomas's touch in any capacity and wasn't above discouraging his desire to do so.

Finally, he'd given up trying to hold her. It was when he could see that her silence was complete, she was mute in his presence whether he touched her or not, that he left. He moved into his own apartment, feeling that she needed time and space to forgive him. Their home became Carla's place and his presence was tolerated, if not openly welcomed.

Carla shook off her reflections. Raising a brow in inquiry, if not outright challenge, she asked, "What?" She needed a good argument to blow off some steam, she thought, looking at Thomas.

It was not that Carla thought she could beat Thomas. That night, two years ago, she had only the element of surprise on her side. She just wanted him to understand she wasn't going to bow down and be kicked like a dog.

Not by him.

Not by anyone.

Two

She laughed into the phone. Her voice was warm honey in his ear. He could feel it seducing him through the receiver. It was barely 7:30 in the morning and already she had him anticipating the evening. “Damn, girl, you’re bad.”

She laughed again. “That’s what you like about me, so why complain?”

His voice was deeper, husky with desire when he spoke again. “Yeah, I like that and a couple of other things, too.”

“No nuts, no fucking glory.”

He smiled into the phone correcting her, “No guts, no glory.”

“No. I meant no motherfucking *nuts*, no motherfucking *glory*.” They both laughed, as he finally picked up her train of thought. “You feel me?” she asked.

“I’m wishing I could right now.”

“We’re still good for tonight? Your watch dog’s going to let you out again and so soon?”

At the mention of Betty Jean, Ezekiel's mood dampened. The passion of just moments before was replaced with another kind of heat when he said, "Betty's straight. She doesn't trip on shit like that. She ain't worried about me going out."

"I guess not. She knows you have to bring your black ass home eventually, right?" Carla didn't even try to keep the acid from her voice. She couldn't stand fucking Betty Jean. *Betty Jean.* Country fucking ass name. The name Carla wasn't any real prize, but it wasn't no *Betty Jean* either.

"No, she doesn't trip on stupid shit, because she knows I'm a grown man," Ezekiel corrected. "Just because we pick up our mail at the same address and share a breakfast table in the morning doesn't mean she owns me. She knows her bills are paid on time and that's all she needs to fucking know or care about. What I do, I do." He shifted gears, increasing speed as he changed lanes on the freeway. His agitation was clearly visible as the silver convertible darted through the gaps in the traffic.

"Damn, little daddy, you don't have to get all hostile and shit. Every time I mention that bitch, you start tripping and flipping the script," she paused for a moment, debating. Part of her wanted to go off and cuss him out good, but she wanted to get out tonight more. Still, she could not keep from pouting, "Every time I bring that girl up, you bite my head off."

"Then why don't you catch a clue, Carla and stop bringing her up? Don't try to talk to me about Betty Jean. I don't sit at home and discuss you with her, why are you always trying to drag her into our conversations? I don't understand that shit. For the last time, Betty Jean isn't any of your fucking business."

Carla pulled the phone away from her ear, staring at it. She looked at the receiver a long moment before speaking into it. "None of my fucking business?" Her voice was calm. Getting out for the night was pushed to the back of her mind by the need to check his conversation. *Who the hell did he think he was talking to, Betty Jean?*

"But her man can call me at seven in the morning to talk about his hard dick? Why didn't you call her with all the nasty shit you had on your mind twenty minutes ago? Or better yet, you could have just rolled over and fucked her before you got out of bed. You said you wake up ready to go. I don't know, I don't sleep next to you at night. I only get whatever little funky ass time you can steal away for me and that rarely includes a sleepover. You weren't even in your car when you started dialing my number a little while ago. Why didn't you just go back in the goddamned house and ask her to suck your fucking dick or something?"

"Carla, stop tripping, damn. I called you because I wanted to get with you. Like you said, she was right there. Had I wanted her this conversation wouldn't even be taking place. And aside from all that, I called you because you were blowing my cell phone up last night. Even though I keep asking you not to do that shit."

"I wouldn't have to blow you up if you'd stay at my house sometimes, instead of just coming through when you want some pussy. The only time you stay over is when you mad at old girl."

Ezekiel sighed heavily into the phone. Carla was working his nerves. He had to keep telling her the same shit over and over. It wasn't like it was a new situation that kept changing. It wasn't and it *wasn't*. It wasn't a new situation and it damn sure wasn't going to change. He was with Betty Jean and would stay with Betty Jean. He loved her more than his own life. He was with Betty Jean when he met Carla, and would be with her when Carla was only a memory that made him smile. But in the interim, he said, yet again, "Carla, I stay with you when I can. I went fishing last month and spent the weekend holed up with you, remember? She knows I don't like that shit enough to do it that often. I can't step out and post up with you every weekend. I'm not trying to mess up my home life like that. Like I said, I stay with you when I can."

"I know." She tried to sound contrite, but she knew she failed when he cut her off.

Snapping with irritation, he said, "Look, why do I have to keep reassuring you, Carla? I cut for you. We're cool and all that, but damn, I don't know what you want from me. I didn't think we'd kick it for as long as we have, but shit, I don't know what to say to you when you start tripping. Betty Jean isn't going any-fucking-where. It's not like she's a surprise or anything, I told you about BJ before we even exchanged phone numbers. She and I have been through too much for me to just leave her and I don't plan to anyway, I love her. But that doesn't have anything to do with you and me or what we have going on. Why are you always starting up some shit over this?"

"I don't know," she pouted into the phone. Zeke's voice had softened with his last question and she could tell he was trying to make up. She really didn't have an answer for his question. She didn't know why she always fucked with him about his girl. True, she did hate the bitch, but she didn't have to express it verbally or so frequently. "So, what spot do I fill with you, since you love her and aren't planning to leave?"

"A different one."

"Which one?"

"A different one, Carla." He tried to sound firm; he wanted to end the game. Shit, he was getting tired of trying to please everyone. More and more he was feeling backed into corners and pulled apart.

"Your G-spot, player?" Carla switched from pouting child, to purring kitten. She was always wise enough to know when to throw her cards on the table. Zeke was getting angry. Some days he'd listen to her talk shit and some days he turned the tables on her. She'd be the one back peddling and trying to soothe him instead of vice versa.

"What you said isn't true either. What I feel about you isn't just about sex. I like being around you. You're a cool little female to kick it with."

"How come we've never met up without you getting in me, then?" She asked the question with a smile in her voice and he responded in kind. A wide smile spread across his handsome features, smoothing out the deep crease in his forehead.

"Because I'll start thinking about what you do to me and I can't stop myself from wanting more. Or you'll have on some shit that makes my dick hard looking at you and it's over. Damn, girl, you know how sexy you are without even trying. Then when you're trying to do it," he let his voice trail off, pushing air through his teeth in appreciation. "But let me go, ole nasty girl, I'm at work. I'll see you about five-thirty." Ezekiel disconnected the call as he pulled into the parking garage. Spaces were hard to come by and he needed to be on the lookout.

**

Sheila entered the office quietly. Betty Jean had a fantastic view from her office and it was common to find her as she was now, in her chair facing the window. Her fingers were brought together, forming a steeple under her chin. Her eyes were closed. She opened them when she felt her assistant standing before her desk. Placing a finger to her lips, Betty Jean pointed at the headset that hugged her thick hair. "Just a moment, please, Mr. Grailton." She pushed a button on her desk phone and removed the headset.

"Did someone sneak in a few extra hours on us today? I can't believe it's only four o'clock. What's up?"

"Your honey just called. I told him you were on another line, but he didn't want to wait. Your day had too many hours and his didn't have enough, because he's working late. Last minute stuff. Sounded rather pissed about it, too. Speaking of which, I'm going to the ladies room. Man the phone, please, 'cause I ain't out there." Sheila turned and left the office in a brisk swirl of moss green.

Betty Jean smiled at Sheila's retreating back. "Not a problem, as long as no one calls." She replaced the headset, once again clicking the button on the phone. "Hello, Mr. Grailton, I'm sorry about that. No, sir, what I was explaining is that the funds would be lo— Mr. Grailton, you aren't listening to me." Betty Jean turned her chair back to the window, letting the view absorb her tension. Gerald Grailton was always the same. He asked for advice, then fought it hard. He would eventually sign the document, but not without a debate and a great deal of hand-holding.

He really was too old to be handling his own affairs. Betty Jean figured he kicked up a fuss as often as he did just to get attention. She knew he would act this way, he always did. She also knew he would follow her advice eventually. He trusted her completely. He was just a lonely old man who enjoyed an occasional skirmish. But the debate still gave her a headache.

There was a soft glow coming from the living room windows when Ezekiel pulled into the driveway that night. He was tired. As usual, Carla had beat him down and worn him out. She put it on him good tonight, he thought, smiling. His male ego demanded stroking, as well, so he conceded that he had given as good as he'd got. If not better. A shiver ran through him and he shook it off. Damn, she made his toes curl! He shook his head, trying to remove images of Carla's perfectly curved form from his mind.

She was small, maybe five feet tall, but he wasn't certain. She had the smallest waist he'd ever seen. He could nearly circle it with his two hands, but then, at six two, he had large hands. Carla's breasts seemed to fit into them just right. Nice firm grapefruits. Her navel was pierced to draw attention to her abs, which were tight. She had a daughter but her stomach was flat as a wash-board, well muscled and nary a stretch mark in sight.

Her skin was a creamy chocolate. Not yellow boned; not fresh off the boat, either, but a nice smooth shade of cocoa brown. Her body was blemish free, except for her piercings and tattoos. She had *a lot* of piercings. There were the holes that dotted her left earlobe from tip to tip, then the three in her right. One in her left eyebrow and nostril, both tits, her clit and navel. Yes, she had a lot of piercings, Zeke thought. Sixteen. He'd counted once. And they all looked erotic.

She only had two tattoos. He was glad of that. The piercings were one thing, but he hated a woman that was tatted up like a man with one on her hip, thigh, calf, forearm, back and shoulder. Ridiculous. Carla's were cool, though. Only the privileged who saw her naked knew she had two. She had one that stretched across the small of her back, dipping into the waist-band of her clothes. It was a setting sun with the script *It Does!* scrawled beneath it. She said she'd gotten it because she'd always been told that she thought the sun rose and set on her. She said she figured the tattoo would clear up the misunderstanding that it didn't.

The other tattoo was of the masks, Comedy and Tragedy. One's laughing, the other's crying. The script surrounding the masks read: *Make ya laugh: Make ya cry.* It was located on her right side in the pelvic area, where her pelvis and thigh met. The band of her low rise underwear covered it from view. She said the masks were to remind her that the thing you love the most can become the thing you hate with your whole heart. The hand that holds you up the highest, is the same hand that can bring you to your lowest point. She said she had to learn that lesson the hard way and didn't desire a repeat performance. The lesson had been beaten into her and she wasn't likely to forget, but the tattoo was a warning just the same.

She wouldn't go into detail on what the lesson was, how it had been beaten into her, who'd administered it or any of the other particulars, so he hadn't pressed her. She only said that she'd gotten the tattoo about two years ago. He figured it had something to do with her baby's daddy's sorry ass, so he let it go. He couldn't figure out how she ever hooked up with a cat like that anyway. Fucking loser. He knew Carla would tell him the story behind the tattoo someday, when she wanted to talk about it. If not, that was fine, too. He wasn't trying to get involved.

He sighed deeply, breathing Carla in one last time. He got out of the Mustang, locking the door by remote. As he walked up the path to the house, he noticed the light coming from the living room windows flickered occasionally. He frowned at the oddity, before realizing that candles lit the downstairs windows, not electricity. He paused on the front steps before letting himself in. The last thing he needed was Betty Jean trying to seduce him.

Betty Jean came towards him from the kitchen, smiling. Tonight she wore her long hair pinned up, exposing her neck. She left soft tendrils to hang down around her ears, the way he liked. Sophisticated, but sexy.

She wore a sheer shell pink baby doll with a matching mid thigh length robe which she left open. The sash hung drunkenly from its loops at her waist. The baby doll tied together in the front across her chest, then fell away to expose her stomach and the matching thong bottom. Even had he been blind and not able to see the enticing figure she presented, Betty Jean assaulted his other senses, as well. She was wearing *Allure*, a scent that never failed to weaken his knees. It filled the living room, pulling at him.

She stopped walking when she stood directly in front of him. She grabbed his shoulders, pulling him towards her for a kiss. "I'm glad you're home," she breathed the words before her lips touched his. She'd sipped a couple of glasses of wine while she was cooking dinner and waiting for him to arrive, now she had a slight buzz and was feeling good. She deepened the kiss, opening her mouth fully to his. Betty Jean sensed a brief hesitation before he responded. *Maybe she imagined the hesitation,* she mused. Maybe she surprised him. She wasn't often the aggressor, but tonight she wanted him.

Betty Jean ran her hands across Ezekiel's back. She loved the powerful way his body felt beneath her palms. She slid up to him, pulling him closer until there was nothing between them but clothing and his growing erection. She looked down, smiling. *Good, big boy is awake.* Looking at Zeke's face, she said, "I've been waiting for you." She rose up on tiptoe, kissing him quickly on the lips before releasing him.

"I can see that," he replied, his voice thick in his throat. She stood staring at him with big shining brown eyes. She was so sweet. He reached out a hand, touching the hair that had escaped its pins. It was so soft, silky.

"I love you, BJ." The words were not intended, but came unbidden from somewhere within his heart and he meant them. He loved Betty Jean completely. He could not fathom his life without her. She *had* to be in his life. Not just as his friend or someone he spoke with every now and then, but by his side, walking with him. He was going to marry her one day, his BJ. He had no doubts. If he ever jumped the broomstick, it would be her hand he was holding when he landed.

Sometimes he didn't know if she would have him. If she still loved him. Often he doubted it. He'd think he'd crossed the line one too many times or that he'd put her through too much shit, but then she'd look at him with her whole heart showing like she was doing now.

She reached for his hand walking towards the kitchen. "Come see what I did for you."

He could smell the steaks; even before he saw them and he shook his head, returning to his thoughts. *Or* she wouldn't have to look at him at all. She wouldn't have to say a word. She'd just come in from a hard day at work and cook for him and he'd know how she felt. He'd know she still cared for him. Betty Jean always went above and beyond. Always.

Yes, it was times like these when he knew she still loved him. Even if she didn't reply when he told her he loved her. No matter how often he said it there was never any response of *I love you, too.* She would only look at him and smile, but she never said the words back to him. It hadn't always been that way. He could remember a time when she would call him at work just to say she loved him. She would write it on the bathroom mirror sometimes, before she left the house in the morning. They were once the last words on her lips each night, but not anymore. It had been nearly a year or more since she'd let the words cross her lips, but he still knew how she felt for him. It was in everything that she did.

Thinking about all she'd done that evening with him in mind, his conscience began to bother him a little. He wished he would have known what she had planned. He would have canceled his evening with Carla. *Good as it had been.* He could tell Betty Jean wanted him. He could still make love to her, even after Carla. He looked at Betty Jean appreciatively. She had a nice body and it looked damned good in what she was wearing. He imagined the feel of her against him. Hot. Tight. He felt himself harden further and turned abruptly from the kitchen. He needed to bathe.

"Are you going to shower before you eat?" She asked the question to his retreating back. The inquiry was a test, so that she could get an idea of what to expect for the night. Ezekiel was a creature of habit. If he took his shower now, his mind was properly aligned with hers and she had a chance. If he waited and took his shower later, after he ate, she didn't. He would eat, shower, then go to bed, claiming to be wiped out by the day. Eliminating any opportunity for sex. But if he showered now, when they retired upstairs later, he'd be ready. Nothing to do but get in bed and get to it. She tingled with anticipation.

When he responded that he was headed towards the shower, she let out the breath she hadn't realized she held. Maybe no one had claimed his time after work. Maybe he really did work late. For a moment, Betty Jean felt guilty. She had a way of always thinking the worst. Whenever Ezekiel called to say he was working late, she wondered if he told the truth. He'd lied to her so many times. She had no way of knowing if he was still at the office or not. The company phones transferred automatically at five-fifteen. The only way to reach him after that was by cell and she never called that phone. Never. Not for any reason. She remembered too vividly what happened the last time she called his cell phone. It was four years ago, but the incident played itself out in her mind as though it happened yesterday.

She'd been at the house, bored. Ezekiel had gone out, but said he'd make it an early night. He just felt like having a drink or two with the fellas. After a few hours of playing solitaire, she called him, wondering how much longer he'd be. Maybe they could rent a movie. She was going to go crazy if she didn't find something to do. By the third ring, she figured he couldn't hear the phone ringing and she'd leave a message. He'd call back when he listened to it. Maybe he could just bring a movie home and she wouldn't have to get dressed. She was bored stiff, but didn't feel like going out.

When the ringing stopped, Betty Jean waited patiently for Ezekiel's voice to cheerfully request that she leave a message. Instead of Ezekiel's deep baritone, she heard, "Thank you, baby. That ringing was throwing my rhythm off."

There was silence for a moment, then a sharp intake of breath. "Shit." The word was held onto and drug out slowly. "Nothing's wrong with your rhythm, believe me." There was a giggle, followed almost immediately by a moan.

"Take this shit off and come here." Zeke's voice. Thick and strangled. Betty Jean's breath caught in her throat. She didn't know why she hadn't hung up as soon as she realized what she was hearing, but she didn't. Obviously, Ezekiel was meaning to silence the ringer on his phone, not answer the call. It was throwing someone's rhythm off. Horrified, Betty Jean gripped the receiver with both hands, willing it to be a mistake. Maybe she'd dialed the wrong number. Maybe that wasn't Zeke's voice she heard. She was beginning to tremble uncontrollably, but she couldn't make herself hang up the phone.

She remained frozen, listening to a conversation she didn't want to hear. She listened as someone else shrieked Ezekiel's name, followed by a "Please big daddy." Was the woman crying? The voice was a mixture of pleasure and pain as the unknown female pleaded with *big daddy*. "Turn over," Betty Jean heard *big daddy* instruct, followed by a faint smacking sound. "Hurry up."

A feminine moan, then —

"Damn, Sasha, you taste so —"

Finally, she found the strength to hang up. Frantically, she pushed the end call button, effectively cutting off the rest of his sentence. The fact that he even knew what someone else tasted like was more than enough information. It was too much. She didn't require the specifics. She'd ended the call, but she couldn't stop the flow of images from parading through her mind.

Her Ezekiel rubbing someone else's thighs. Him kneeling between them. Kissing her. She squeezed her eyes shut, trying to block out the image, but she couldn't. It was embedded on her mind forever. Ezekiel giving pleasure to someone else. Holding her, touching her, sucking her pussy, no less! Tears poured from her eyes. She hurt so much, she didn't want to believe that Ezekiel could betray her so completely.

Betty Jean moved out of their apartment the next morning. Ezekiel went to work and when he returned she was gone. It took him three weeks to find her and another month after that before he could get her to speak to him. Another two months passed before she would look him in the face, instead of staring at a button on his shirt or at his shoes. It had taken a good year before she would even remotely consider going out with him again.

That was a long time ago, though. They'd been back together for over two years now. In their house for one and dealing with Carla for at least half of that time. Carla came to her mind once again in the same fashion that she always did. Unanticipated. Uninvited. Unwanted. At least, she was unwanted by her, Betty Jean corrected. Ezekiel Johnson didn't seem to have any such problems; especially, if you went by the frequency to which he made up excuses not to be intimate with Betty Jean.

She tried to shake off the sudden anger her wayward thoughts had evoked. Ezekiel was home. Sasha was years ago. Carla was just a nuisance and he was in the shower. Tonight was her night with her man and she wasn't going to let the tramp that was screwing him mess it up. She went to the bottom of the staircase, called for Ezekiel, then turned to set the table. He came down a few minutes later in his boxer shorts and a white cotton tee shirt, smelling strongly of Dove soap.

Betty Jean forced herself to sit calmly through their meal. She enjoyed cooking for him, but as she sipped the last of her wine, food was the last thing on her mind. She observed Zeke across the small Queen Anne-styled table. He was a handsome devil. His was a deep caramel complexion. He weighed a nice two hundred and twenty-two pounds that complimented his height well. He wore his hair cut low, not faded, just low. He sported a mustache that connected with a goatee and he kept both neatly trimmed. Rimless glasses framed intelligent brown eyes that looked nearly gold in certain light, as they did now with the flame from the candles dancing in them. She tried to hide her smile. It was going to be a good night.

After eating a second helping of food and polishing off an entire serving of canned fruit, Ezekiel excused himself to the bedroom as she tidied up the kitchen. Wiping the counters down and placing the remaining food in storage dishes for the refrigerator, Betty Jean turned off the lights in the kitchen. She blew out the candles she had placed around the living room, as she passed them. Making an effort not to run, she went upstairs to join Zeke.

He was in the bathroom when she entered the room, so Betty Jean took the opportunity to spray her negligee lightly with perfume. She selected the CD she wanted to hear, picked up the remote and climbed into bed. She arranged her pillows while the deep rhythms of the song she selected enveloped the room. The four glasses of wine she'd consumed pulled her into the song and she closed her eyes, giving into the beat. Smiling. Waiting. Anticipating the conclusion of her evening and the things she would do with her man. She was so deeply embedded in her fantasies; the CD was on its fourth song before she realized Zeke still hadn't come into the bedroom. He was still in the bathroom.

He climbed into bed in the middle of the fifth song, holding his stomach. He removed his glasses and lay back, closing his eyes. His hand still cradled his stomach and Betty Jean was getting an ugly feeling in the pit of hers. "Turn your music down a little, Sweetie," he said weakly, patting her thigh. "I don't know what's wrong with my stomach. I feel horrible."

"Do you need me to get something for you?" she asked quietly, not because she believed that anything was wrong with his stomach other than the fact that he was full of shit, but because she could feel he expected it of her. So, she played along and read her line.

Mentally, she ad libbed, *Could I find your integrity for you, you lying dog? Your conscience, perhaps? Your love for me that runs so deep it allows you to fuck some other woman then lie in my face and deny me? Faithless swine.* Betty Jean's mind reeled with accusations. She wanted to confront him for the lying, cheating, jackass she knew him to be. She wanted to, but she couldn't. What if she were wrong? What if he really did feel ill? She didn't know if his stomach ache was a ruse or not. She didn't even know for certain if there was another woman. She had no concrete evidence that he was involved with anyone *this time*. The only proof she had that Carla Jeffries even existed was her caller ID box. And she'd seen Carla's number long ago; at least seven months earlier. Ezekiel was on vacation and nearly every day that week, when she'd come home from work there'd be an anonymous caller on the ID. She'd pressed star six nine a couple of time when it was the last phone number on the ID and it was always the same message. *You've reached Carla Jeffries, I'm not in.* Betty Jean would hang up before the message finished. But again, that was months ago. Maybe Ezekiel had already grown tired of Carla and Betty Jean only imagined that he was still doing wrong.

Betty Jean tried, as usual, to convince her mind to eat the bullshit her heart wanted to feed her. As usual, it did no good. She knew Carla still existed. He'd just cleaned up his act and stopped being so sloppy. She didn't have concrete, solid evidence that she could hold in her hand, but she didn't need any. She *knew* her man. He wasn't yet done playing with Carla. Or her either, it seemed. Especially not her.

Ezekiel shook his head from side to side on the pillow, declining her offer of assistance. "I'm going to just lay here. Maybe try to get some sleep." He turned his head on the pillow and burrowed into it slightly, as if to illustrate his discomfort. "Your music, baby," he reminded.

Betty Jean raised the remote, turning off the stereo system. She wanted to raise her pillow over his head and snuff out the truth. Instead, she touched the base on the bedside lamp, turning off the dim light. She sighed heavily into the darkness. "Hurts like a son of a bitch," she heard him mumble beside her.

"I know the feeling well," she replied, turning onto her side. Her back to his performance. Keeping to her ritual, she began to recite her prayers, careful to confess her sins. Long slow hours crawled by before she was able to fall asleep.

Three

She woke to the feel of Ezekiel's hands sliding across her body. Still more asleep than awake, she moaned deeply. The feel of his hands in her present state of unconsciousness was exquisite. His hands were quickly followed by his mouth, so she turned onto her back giving him better access to her body. He pulled the ties on her negligee, releasing the bow. He kissed each breast as it was exposed to him. His tongue licked her right nipple to a sharp point, while teasing the left one with his fingertips. Soon Betty Jean found herself spreading her legs for his other hand. In no time at all, she was fully awake, trembling from the mounting pleasure Ezekiel was giving her.

She'd been waiting for his touch for so long, he barely brushed her flesh with the ball of his thumb and she was squirming on the bed. She bit her lip to keep from screaming his name.

Her hips lifted from the bed, seeking what his fingers promised. But he wasn't ready to give her what she wanted. When his mouth trailed hot kisses down her body, pausing briefly at her navel, before replacing his hand, she raised from the bed completely. He caught her hips with his hands, keeping her pinned to his lips as he sucked and pulled at her clitoris. When she at last relaxed in his hold, limp from her release, the long length of his body covered hers.

He slid up her body between her legs. Wrapping them tightly around his waist, he entered her. Ezekiel made love to Betty Jean slowly. He was in no hurry, as he enjoyed the feel of her, not allowing himself to climax until she clawed at him for the third time that night. He could feel her tightening and convulsing around his shaft. He climbed higher, plunging deeper into her, reaching for her womb before releasing his seed. Collapsing beside her, he kissed her shoulder, pulling the covers across their naked bodies. Betty Jean sighed deeply, snuggling into her pillow. Ezekiel's arms were around her and they felt so good. He felt good. She lay back thinking of what they'd just done and a smile touched her lips. Filled to overflowing with contentment, she picked up the right hand that held her breast and kissed it.

Lord, she loved her man, she thought dreamily and closed her eyes to sleep once again.

**

This time it wasn't Zeke's hands that woke her but his cell phone. It was ringing incessantly. It was on the night stand and he was in the bathroom.

Carla.

Betty Jean didn't even have to look at the thing to know it would be her. She stretched, remembering the early morning hours, and smiled. She didn't care if Carla did call this morning. Ezekiel showed her where his feelings were. There's no way he could have done what he did a few hours ago, with such depth of feeling, if Carla meant anything to him. There was no way Carla could receive what she and Zeke gave to one another. Right? He loved her; shared his life with her, *Betty Jean.* Carla was just a momentary distraction that he would lose interest in just like the others.

They were just about sex. Ezekiel didn't bring his heart to the bed when he was with Carla. *Did he*? she asked herself, seeking assurance she couldn't give. No, Betty Jean shook her head firmly. Ezekiel, her Ezekiel, did not give Carla the same thing he gave her. She injected confidence into her inner voice. Carla only had his body periodically, not his heart. She couldn't know the ecstasy Betty Jean experienced in Zeke's embrace. When he touched Betty Jean it was with love, which added to the pleasure of the act. Carla couldn't have shared that with him. *Could she*? Betty Jean asked herself, not certain she wanted an answer.

**

They looked at one another smiling.

Carla lay draped across Ezekiel fighting to catch her breath. "I don't want to move."

His hands rubbed her back. "Then don't."

"I have to get up if you're going back to work. You've been here for almost an hour already."

He hunched his shoulders, pulling her closer. "My laptop is in the car. As long as I have it with me, I'm at work."

"Oh, I forgot, you're Mr. Big Businessman." Carla nipped lightly at his shoulder.

"Technical writer."

"Same thing," she said, sliding one leg across his body until she straddled him.

Ezekiel's hands slid down her back, stopping instinctively at her tattoo. His fingers traced the design by memory.

"What's your girl do?" Carla asked, resting her chin on his shoulder. His hands stopped stroking her. He made to rise from beneath her, but she tightened her thighs. "Relax, little daddy. I feel too good to start a fight. I was just wondering if she was like you, all big business and shit. Just trying to check out the competition."

He was silent for so long, she thought he wasn't going to answer. He put an arm around Carla's waist, holding her to him. He never liked talking about his girl. "Her job is better than mine."

"Did you meet her in college?" Carla asked the question, visualizing the two of them studying together in Ezekiel's dorm room, then fooling around after. She didn't know if he lived on campus when he went to college, but it suited her fantasy. She tried not to feel jealous.

"No."

"Did you guys go to the same college?"

Ezekiel sighed. "Betty Jean went to two different universities. She completed her Bachelors degree at one place, received her first Masters from somewhere else, then went back to her first alma mater for her second Masters. No, we didn't attend school together. I don't even have a Masters degree, just the Bachelors. Can we not talk about her, please?" he asked. He'd said his narrative about Betty Jean in the driest of tones, hoping to dissuade further conversation.

Carla frowned. Leaning forward, she bit at his chin. "What the fuck is an alma mater?"

"The school someone attends is their alma mater."

"So, Miss Betty Jean has two alma maters? How nice." Carla's tone was level, but the words still dripped with heavy sarcasm.

"Why are you bringing her up right now anyway?" Ezekiel asked, irritated by Carla's topic of choice.

"Because I just finished getting dug out by her man and I was wondering about her, that's all. She has a tendency to pop into my mind when I'm with you."

"You're a mood killer, Carla." He tried to dislodge her again, but she held on tight.

"Okay, okay," she said kissing his neck. She moved her hips against him, sighing against his skin. "We don't have to talk about your girl. In fact, let's not talk about anything."

He reached for her head, kissing her.

**

She'd gotten her weekend off to a good start. It had been weeks since she let the specter of Carla haunt her. Ezekiel hadn't worked late, hung out with the boys, or been otherwise unaccounted for since the night she'd tried to seduce him. Not once had he called to say he was running late. Nothing unexpected came up. Even his weekends were saved for Betty Jean. They'd gone to dinner and for drinks a few times. They even drove out to the lake a couple of Saturdays ago, because he knew how she loved being near the water. She'd gone to get her hair done and run a few errands. When she returned home, Zeke surprised her with the trip to the lake. He came through the front door about ten minutes behind her, carrying a huge picnic basket. They'd driven to the lake and had a wonderful evening.

And their nights together were phenomenal. Goodness, she couldn't count how many times he'd made her call the Lord's name in vain. And she hadn't needed to seduce him, either. Their sex was more incredible every time he held her. Each time Ezekiel made love to her, she could feel him pouring more of his heart into her, binding them more firmly together.

She picked up one of Zeke's colored shirts from the basket and tossed it into the washing machine that had just begun to agitate. She could still smell his cologne clinging faintly to the cotton fabric and closed her eyes for a second, daydreaming.

Betty Jean shook her head with a smile and reached into the basket removing a pair of black running shorts. She checked the clothing as Ezekiel had a terrible habit of putting his clothes in the wash basket without emptying the pockets. Betty Jean was sure his pockets were only checked when she did it, regardless of how heatedly Zeke disputed the charge. She never failed to discover something left behind on wash day. Finding a neatly folded twenty dollar bill, she shook her head, smiling again. She placed the money on the hood of the dryer before throwing the shorts into the churning water.

She continued sorting through the clothes, tossing the whites aside for later and placing the dark clothes in the machine. She always did the dark clothes first. There was a hidden fear in the back of her mind about getting chlorine on her clothes and ruining them. She habitually washed the dark clothes first before she even touched the bleach bottle. She wasn't certain where the notion came from but it wasn't anything new. She'd had this *laundry phobia* since she first started washing clothes. Another of her concerns was stray socks. Betty Jean learned a long time ago that just because a set went in, didn't mean you'd get a set back. Which was why she always pinned her socks together. She'd either lose both of them or none at all. She assumed it was working; she hadn't lost a sock in years. Picking a safety pin from the bowl on the dryer, she neatly secured the socks in her hand before they, too, were tossed in, then drug beneath the dark surface of the water.

She snagged a pair of Ezekiel's slacks from the basket, debating whether or not they should go to the cleaners. Deciding against it, she dug into the pockets for forgotten treasures. Her fingers closed around stubs from a parking garage. She threw them atop the dryer with the other contents from Zeke's pockets. Placing the remaining clothes into the washer, she added a final scoop of detergent before closing the lid and placing the empty basket on top of the machine. Betty Jean picked up the second basket which was filled with the folded clothes from her first load. Balancing the basket on her hip as she scooped up Ezekiel's forgotten things from the dryer top, she walked from the pantry.

When she first noticed how often Ezekiel neglected checking his pockets, she converted a coffee can into her Washer Money can. At the end of the month they usually used the funds to dine out. She pulled the coffee can from its place on the bookshelf in the room and pushed the folded currency through the tiny slit in the lid. She'd found a miniature Phillips screwdriver in a shirt pocket. She had no idea what he could have been doing with it. She set it aside to return to his tool box later.

Betty Jean was sorting through the debris, mentally labeling it all trash, when something caught her attention. When she first removed the stubs from Ezekiel's pockets, she thought them to be the kind they give you at parking garages for validation, but she was wrong.

Betty Jean picked up one of the square tickets, turning it over slowly in her hand. Movie tickets. The parking stubs weren't for parking at all. They were stubs from a movie Ezekiel had gone to see. A movie she couldn't possibly have seen because she was under the hair dryer at Edna's House of Elegance at eleven-fifteen two Saturdays past. Nope, there was no way in hell she'd been at a matinee, but apparently Ezekiel had and he needed two tickets. Betty Jean sighed, letting her shoulders droop sadly. So, that explained the trip to the lake Saturday evening. *And the beautiful picnic*, her hurt feelings hastily added.

He'd been wanting to do something special for her, he'd said as he spread food across the checkered blanket. She marveled when he pulled each new tasty treat from the basket, exclaiming how much she was enjoying his surprise. She could still see his perfect mouth smiling.

Been planning to do this for a long time. You deserve this sort of treatment, Betty Jean. They were sweet words that had her blushing before he was even finished speaking and he looked so sincere. Now she read a different meaning into his words. Instead of his planning a lovely picnic to surprise her, he'd been planning her deception. And fool that she was she'd bought it. Hook, line and sinker. He'd probably only picked up the picnic basket on his way home to explain his absence. But she was a fool that never questioned him, anyway. She shook her head sadly; he was right. She did deserve this sort of treatment. Had he intended the irony of his words when he said them? Was he even then thinking her a fool?

The glow that had been surrounding Betty Jean for the last several weeks faded, leaving no trace that it had ever been there at all. She sat on the edge of the bed, the ticket stubs in her hand. She stared at them through a curtain of tears that she would not let fall. She was so fucking sick of crying over Ezekiel Johnson. Betty Jean took a deep breath, opening her lungs to the passage of air. She sat on the bed, dejected, letting her self pity at being betrayed again by Ezekiel consume her. It was in the middle of this new anguish, this fresh deceit, that Betty Jean realized the significance of the ticket stubs. And her pain magnified.

Ezekiel may have taken someone to the movies – *someone?* Of course it was Carla. Betty Jean just didn't want to admit it yet. There was a bigger picture coming into focus and she held the evidence in her hand. Betty Jean wished it were a someone. Some anonymous nobody that he hadn't spent nearly half a year screwing. But, again, she knew it was Carla. Carla whom Ezekiel was only supposed to be having sex with.

Betty Jean and Ezekiel were on their way to the lake before two o'clock. He'd been to see a movie that started at eleven-fifteen, which left a small window of time. He'd taken Carla to a show, but sex hadn't been included in their date. There hadn't been enough time.

When she left the house at ten-thirty that morning, Ezekiel was still at home. There hadn't been time for sex before the movie or after, as Zeke went to the grocery store on his way home. No, she was certain of it. There was an indescribable knot of fear in her stomach that told her she was right. There had only been time for a show. The realization made Betty Jean feel worse. A date without sex put Carla in a different league. It gave the relationship more significance. Carla was no longer someone he only used for sex. A silly distraction that he would eventually grow tired of. She was now more than that. She was someone Ezekiel wanted to spend time with. And the only reason you spend time with someone is to get to know them. *Why was Ezekiel trying to get to know Carla?* Betty Jean's mind demanded.

She'd had always seen Carla as what she was, a booty call, but now she held proof that Carla was more than that. It wasn't necessary to wine, dine or entertain side-pussy. Not when the situation was understood. When you knew you were only pussy on the side, a spare tire for when something was wrong with the original. But there was a big difference between having a spare tire to use and driving two separate vehicles.

Ezekiel was driving two separate vehicles.

Betty Jean was scared. Her mind was racing. Zeke had taken Carla to see a movie and that was the extent of it. He'd wanted to spend time with Carla before going to the lake with Betty Jean. The implications of such an act were colossal in her mind and try as she might, she couldn't shake them. What did Zeke's actions mean? Did he spend their evening together by the water thinking about Carla? Had Carla gone with him to pick out the picnic? How often did they spend time together just hanging out?

Betty Jean got up from the bed. She returned to the bathroom. Tearing the stubs up, she flushed the pieces down the toilet. She watched them disappear, wishing all her problems could be disposed of so easily. She wished she could call Zeke and talk to him. She wished suddenly that he was home, but he was gone for the day. He'd left to go fishing around three that morning and wasn't expected back until sometime on Sunday. Betty Jean sighed, heavily. She'd be dead by then, her heart hurt so much.

**

"What are we doing tonight?"

"What we do every night, Pinky," he echoed the popular cartoon, smiling.

She laughed, hitting his arm. "You aren't funny. Come on now, tell me so I know how hard to fight to get off work on time tonight."

At her words, Ezekiel sat up abruptly. "Why didn't you take the day off? You knew I was spending this weekend with you, Carla, damn! You bitch about me spending time with you, then when I do, you won't even take off from work."

Carla smiled. It was difficult not to roll her eyes to the ceiling. Zeke had a way of acting as though she existed for his amusement alone. She retrieved her cigarillo from the ashtray and relit it. She leaned back, taking a long drag before blowing the smoke out at her leisure, saying, "I don't have a career, motherfucker. My shit does not come to a screeching halt at five p.m. Friday. I have a goddamned job and I am at that shit daily. Day, night, weekends. It doesn't matter. I have rent to pay." She raised a brow at the mention of her rent.

"What? Why are you looking at me like that? Get that fool you let run up in here anytime he wants to, to pay your rent. Hell, he should be doing that anyway, since you have a daughter together. Sorry ass. I don't know why you women like dudes like that," he complained, shaking his head.

Carla clenched the cigarillo between her teeth and rolled from the bed. She needed to shower before work and she used the turn in topics as an excuse to get up. She hated it when Zeke talked about Thomas. He didn't know shit about Thomas, but was always quick to say something negative about him. Thom didn't live with her. He had his own rent to pay and he was always there for her and their shorty. Without a doubt, without question. She refused his offered help routinely. She could pay her own bills. So, Ezekiel really needed to shut the fuck up when it came to Thomas. He didn't know a goddamned thing.

She stepped into the steaming shower, letting the water pour over her. She stood hoping the warm liquid would relax her. Her mind wandered briefly and she wondered if Betty Jean ever had to put up with Zeke's bullshit. She worked the soap into a lather, shaking her head. Probably not. Betty Jean had it easy.

Four

She lay atop the bed, spread eagle, like she was trying to make snow angels on the pale blue sheets. Either that or she was trying to become an angel herself. She looked the part with her hair loose and tangled around her shoulders. She looked like an angel recent from the fall. She'd been lying that way for the past few hours. She was tired. Truly, deeply, tired of the ridiculous game she and Ezekiel were playing. Six years. Six fucking years and he still had a chess board sitting between them, ready to play games and she was tired of it. Tired of pretending that she was as stupid as he obviously thought she was. Tired of proving his assumption correct with her damnable silence.

Why, why, why? Her mind screamed the inquiry in trio. She just couldn't understand why he wouldn't leave. Why was this life of subterfuge preferable to being alone, without her? Why was he trying to drive her insane with his lies and deceit? Why did he want her to hate him, because he was definitely going to make that happen? It was either hate Ezekiel or herself and she'd been hating herself for years now. Every time she allowed him to get away with one of his schemes, she hated the weakness that permitted her to turn her head and swallow her words of resentment. Always assuring herself it would be for the last time. That Ezekiel was going to realize her worth and straighten up. His proposal was just a breath away. She knew it....

Betty Jean tried to go about her day, but the ticket stubs would not leave her mind. She'd driven around aimlessly. She was so deeply immersed in her thoughts and struggles that she kept missing her exits on the freeway. Finally, she'd just given up and gone home.

There was a well of hurt in her chest that ran clear down to her soul. It filled every bit of her until it crowded everything else out and she had nothing left but the pain.

She'd intended to complete the rest of her cleaning, but she found she couldn't. She lacked the strength. It was all she could do to pull herself up the staircase to her room. She'd been dragging around all day with a heavy heart. Its leaden weight was pulling her further down until she didn't have the strength to do anything except fall across the bed.

She'd been doing her best imitation of a snow angel ever since.

She'd sought sleep, like the coward she knew she was, but it eluded her, preferring to take no part in her pity party. She was on her own.

Retrieving the remote from the nightstand, she turned on the CD player and listened as the silky rhythms of the song filled the room, surrounding her. Betty Jean closed her eyes and felt the music wrap itself around her heart. She could feel the hypnotic beat as it began to melt into her defenses. Tears slid from beneath her closed lids, as she began to sing along:

The time is right, I'm going to pack my bags

and take that journey down the road,
'cause over the mountain, I see the bright sunshine
and I want to live inside the glow

She made it through the first stanza before she was forced to stop singing. Her throat closed, refusing to let any more of her anguish seep out to escape with the healing lyrics of the song. Stubbornly, Betty Jean continued to mouth the words. The tears began to fall in earnest, as though they compensated for the loss of her voice. When the song began to fade she pressed the repeat button on the remote, allowing the music to fill the room once again.

Oh, how she wanted to be free.

She wanted to pack her bags and chase the glow, too.

While she could still see it, feel it, believe that it existed somewhere, even if she always seemed to be standing facing towards the light, instead of basking in it. She wanted to run while she still felt that she could reach the sunshine, before she got so fucking tired she'd just lie down and never get up. She felt that way now. Like she couldn't get up; like she didn't even have the will to try.

They had no children. No ties other than the superficial. Nothing that said she couldn't leave him. Nothing that denoted a reason why she simply couldn't walk away from Ezekiel, except that she was weak. She loved Ezekiel with every ounce of who she was. She sometimes thought she was who she was because of loving him. He made her feel invincible. With him, she was fierce, strong, proud. Everything she needed to be to survive this world. Sometimes she thought she was giving Ezekiel too much credit, that he didn't control who she was so completely.

But just now, within the confines of her broken spirit, she knew it to be fact. His love *did* control her. She was lying across her bed feeling battered, broken...*weak* and her condition was a direct result of loving Zeke.

She thought again about all the education she had and wondered why none of her intelligence showed in her relationship. Why with Zeke was she willing to be so damned stupid? She tried to close her mind as she slid back into the song:

> *Please understand, that it's not that I don't care,*
> *but right now these walls are closing in on me*
> *I love you more than I love life itself,*
> *but I need to find a place where I can breathe*

The words washed over her, drowning her in their sweet embrace. She, too, needed a place where she could breathe. Betty Jean took a deep laborious breath and squeezed her eyes shut, mentally visualizing India singing to her alone. The singer assured Betty Jean that someone understood her torment. Her heartache was shared.

**

Zeke could feel Betty Jean's sadness when he entered the house the next evening. He immediately thought of his weekend with Carla and felt the fingers of guilt tapping him roughly on the shoulder. He came into the living room, leaving his things at the door. She wasn't there. He started a quiet search of the house, panic rising in his chest, until he discovered her in their bedroom. She was sitting on the edge of the bed, perfectly still, with her hands folded neatly in her lap. Seeing her sitting there, so broken, with her head hanging down, Ezekiel's eyes burned.

He walked into the room, kneeling before her on the floor. She didn't raise her head, even when he slid his arms around her waist. Instead, she moved her hands to his head and he let it fall into her lap, seeking comfort from the one who needed comforting. Betty Jean smoothed her fingers across his hair, enjoying the texture. She looked down at her fingers that pulled gently on the short springy curls. Her vision blurred and tears fell from beneath her lashes. Her body shook slightly as she tried to contain her sorrow. She felt Zeke's arms tighten around her as he began to kiss her thigh.

He gradually worked his way up her body, stopping to plant tender kisses along the way. It was as if he kissed a bleeding wound, securing it. Soon Betty Jean lay across the bed with Ezekiel's strong body above her. He balanced himself on his arms, keeping his weight off her. He looked into her eyes and held them. She was the dearest thing to his heart and he could feel her pain as if it were his own. The last thing he ever wanted was to hurt her, but once again, he knew he had. Only he could cause Betty Jean such sadness. He wondered if she'd found out where he really spent his weekend. They lay in silence watching one another. Betty Jean could feel him slowly easing her, healing her, lifting the burdens from her heavy heart. She looked into his eyes and could see his love; it was a tangible entity. She didn't know why he did the things he did. Why he hurt her, but she did know that he loved her. It was only she who held his heart. The other women came and went, but he never let go of her. She knew he loved her, but his love hurt.

Zeke's eyes burned hotly, blurring Betty Jean's face. He could barely see her through his clouded vision and the notion distressed him. He imagined life without her and he thought he'd break down right then and there. But then she touched him, sweet and gentle, just like she was. Her hand lifted to cup the side of his face brushing away the wetness he hadn't realized was there. She wiped at his tears with the tips of her fingers, soothing his pain.

Zeke's mouth claimed hers hungrily. The kiss held a savage passion that he had never displayed with her. They made love as if the world would end if they didn't. Betty Jean clawed at Ezekiel, leaving her marks on him. He loved her with abandonment, catching her up in the blaze to join him. He loved her like being inside of her wasn't enough. He sought something. Demanded knowledge only her body held. When it was over they curled into one another. Their limbs each locked around the other, holding on securely for fear of waking up in an empty bed.

It was morning before either of them moved again.

**

He had to let Carla go.

He didn't know if Betty Jean knew about Carla, but she knew something. He remembered what he went through the last time she left him. The confusion. The turmoil. The hurt. He hunted all over the city, but kept coming up empty. It was as though she'd disappeared from the face of the earth. He'd gone to her job and been told she quit. Nearly a month had gone by before he thought to go to Edna's House of Elegance. Betty Jean showed up on his second weekend of staking out the place. He closed his eyes, shaking his head, reliving again the horror of losing her. He felt again the pain and uncertainty. He'd been so afraid he wouldn't find her.

When he finally persuaded her to speak to him, she refused to tell him why she left their apartment. To date it was still a mystery. He'd gone to work, leaving her asleep in bed and when he returned, she was gone. She'd only said cryptically that if she knew why she left, so did he. After all, he was first eye witness to his actions. He translated that to mean Betty Jean found out about Diane or Sasha, the two women he was seeing at the time. Once he found Betty Jean, he broke off communication with them both.

He lacked will power.

He loved Betty Jean, but couldn't make himself stay faithful to her. He'd be good for a month or two, but inevitably he'd regress. It was hard being monogamous. There were so many fine women walking around. The variety was too tempting sometimes and he'd see something he had to taste. Samples at a sweets shop. He couldn't say no.

His phone rang for the fourth time. He continued to ignore it. Carla had been calling him for days now. He should talk to her, but he didn't know how she was going to react to his news. He didn't want her crying and saying how much she loved him like What's-Her-Name had done. He tilted his head to the side in concentration, frowning. What was that girl's name, anyway? Brenda? Barbara? Bobbi? Bobbi, that was it!

When he broke it off with her, she snapped a little bit. She kept calling him, crying into the phone, trying to arrange something. Talking about killing herself. Crazy shit like that. He didn't know what happened to her, but he was glad when she finally gave up on him and stopped calling.

He noticed his phone stopped ringing. There was no flashing envelope, so she hadn't left a message that time. He was only mildly disappointed.

Five

"This is some real bullshit, Ezekiel and you know it," she paused, waiting. For what she didn't know. She reached his voice mail again. "All right. Fuck this. I have enough bullshit," she stressed the word adding a heavy emphasis on the t, "and drama in my life." She paused again, anger making her breathe through her nostrils. Her lips pressed together in a tight line.

After gathering her thoughts, she said, "You ask yourself this. If she couldn't satisfy you before me, how is your sweet Betty Jean going to satisfy you after me? You stupid son-of-a-bitch!" She slammed the phone down before her voice broke, betraying her. Two weeks had passed since she'd heard from Ezekiel. She'd called but hadn't reached him. Left messages, but they went unanswered. He was probably feeling guilty about the weekend they spent together.

He didn't want to hurt Betty Jean.

What kind of shit was that? Fuck Betty Jean. What about her? Carla. How many times had she heard him show concern for Betty Jean's feelings? She guessed he didn't give a shit if she was hurt, crushed, forgotten. Carla brushed the tears from her face with an impatient hand. She couldn't believe she'd given damn near a year of her life to that fuck.

But her eyes were wide open now and she could see through Zeke's lies. He never cared for her. He only gave a fuck about cocooning Betty Jean from injury, even at Carla's expense. Always at Carla's expense. Especially, at Carla's expense. *Come on, I've gotta go, BJ's waiting on me. Naw, not tonight, Betty Jean wants to go do something. I can't stay long, I told Betty Jean I wouldn't be that late.* She always had to sit on the back burner when it came to Betty Jean. She knew that's what his silence was about now, too. Betty Fucking Jean. All he wanted from Carla was what he'd gotten. Good pussy. He used her for sex then went home to his gal. The one he really cared about.

Well, she was fed up. Finished. Done. Fuck Ezekiel Johnson. Betty Jean could have her man back and gladly.

**

Sheila was just biting into her cheeseburger when Betty Jean told her the news. She put her hand in front of her mouth, asking around a mouth filled with food, "You're kidding? They offered you that much? What are you, a small country?" She asked the question incredulously, but she was pleased for her friend. She'd worked with Betty Jean for years and thought she deserved whatever good fortune came her way. She was entitled to each zero in the six figure offer.

Betty Jean laughed. She loved Sheila. She never had to wonder if she meant what she said. Sheila was terribly frank and rarely pulled punches. It was one of the many things that endeared her to Betty Jean. If she took the job in California, Sheila was part of the deal. She couldn't even imagine going without her and that was exactly what she'd told the partner that contacted her. She would love the position, but couldn't dream of taking it without Sheila. She hadn't mentioned that part of the deal to her assistant, yet. Betty Jean was savoring the moment. As genuinely pleased for her as Sheila was, she knew it was going to get even better. Smiling, she told Sheila about the bargain she'd made. She chose to say it just as Sheila sipped her coke. The news sent Sheila's drink down the wrong pipe and she choked, spurting liquid out.

Coughing, eyes watering from the exertion, she shrieked, "Do not play with me, Betty Jean Carlson!" Sheila looked around to the other tables sheepishly; she had not meant to be so loud, but she was shocked by what she'd been told. She smiled at Betty Jean. White teeth in a dark face. "Doubled?" Betty Jean shrugged. "Mine, not yours? Doubled?"

Betty Jean smiled. "If Hurstwode & Donovan want me badly enough to quadruple my salary," saying it out loud, she too was finding it hard to believe, "then surely they'll settle for tripling it and doubling yours. I can't leave without you. I won't even consider the offer unless you come along." It still boggled her mind that they wanted her enough to negotiate terms. Their original salary offer hadn't been her own figure. Hurstwode laid it on the table with the job offer and she merely countered it with something else. Something that included Sheila. They were bringing Betty Jean in at the top. A vice president. No more ladder climbing. Gone were the days of hanging on a rung, waiting to move up. The only slot above hers was Chief Financial Officer, Charles Hurstwode himself.

With Hurstwode & Donovan's offer, Betty Jean had arrived. Everything she'd been cultivating for years was finally coming into fruition. Zeke flashed before her mind's eye and she smiled, nearly purring with contentment. Yes, everything was coming up roses for her. Carla was gone. Zeke's cell phone was no longer ringing non stop, demanding his attention. When he called to say he was working late, she no longer trembled with dread. Her doubts were gone, laid to rest with her fears and she was happy. She could believe in Zeke's word again. She no longer saw each morning as an injustice done just to spite her. She welcomed and embraced them with open arms.

They were even discussing marriage and babies. At night, he would hold her, saying how he couldn't wait to see her swollen with his child, which quickly led to discussions of marriage, as Betty Jean wasn't the type of woman to have a baby without the benefit of a wedding band circling her finger first. She bent the rules far enough by living with Ezekiel, but at least that only affected the two of them. She would require something a hell of a lot more substantial than a verbal understanding before she brought a child into their situation; but for now, she was content. The new job offer cinched her euphoria. In California, they could start fresh, new, with no hidden hurts waiting to jump out at them.

"When did you find out about this? What did Zeke say? Is he going with you? What am I saying?" Sheila tapped her forehead with an open palm. "Of course, he's going!" Sheila's voice pulled Betty Jean from her own thoughts, returning her to the conversation at hand.

"Hurstwode made the offer himself first thing this morning. He called at 7:25, saying he knew I was the type to get an early jump on the day." Betty Jean beamed from the remembered compliment.

"Do you think he noticed that you answered your own phone line?" Sheila asked the question with a mischievous grin on her lips, causing Betty Jean to laugh out loud. While it was Sheila's duty to answer Betty Jean's phone line, Betty Jean was on her own most mornings until a quarter after eight. Only rare occasions would see Sheila seated at her big mahogany desk before then. Because she was quick to volunteer her services, work through lunch or stay late, all without a murmur of complaint, Betty Jean overlooked the fifteen minutes.

She shook her head at the question, saying, "No, I don't think he was paying attention to who answered the phone. I think the test was to see if *I* would be there that early in the morning."

She took a sip from her own soda, answering Sheila's previous question regarding Ezekiel. "I called him a little while ago, but only said that I had one hell of a surprise for him tonight when I get home."

"What'd he say?" Sheila asked, sipping what was left of her cola.

Betty Jean blushed, answering in an imitation of Zeke's deeper tones, "*I can be there in twenty minutes if you don't mind it quick.*"

"Nasty ass."

Betty Jean's blush deepened. "He's been like that lately. I don't know what's come over him."

Sheila laughed, chewing the end of her straw. "I was talking about you, bitch." A light breeze blew in keeping the air from being too stiff and the two sat on the restaurant's covered verandah enjoying the southern sun. Their hour for lunch was drawing to a rapid close, but they lingered, the mood light, with the news from Hurstwode & Donovan. Betty Jean ordered refills on their soft drinks and the two women continued their mini celebration.

**

"California?"

"California." She nodded her head in confirmation for the second time. She was fighting to keep a straight face, but it was proving difficult. She couldn't help it. The expression on Ezekiel's face was priceless. She thought he'd be surprised, but he was shocked. It was too yummy a prospect and she was thoroughly enjoying his response. Betty Jean slid from her seat until she kneeled on the soft carpet before him. With her body holding his knees apart, she took his face in her hands and kissed him softly.

"Surprised?"

He shook his head, dazed. "I can't believe they made you this offer. HD is one of the largest finance companies in the United States and they're growing fast internationally, as well." He shook his head again. "And they came to you, baby. It's an incredible offer, BJ, I'm proud of you." He wrapped his arms loosely around her waist, kissing her forehead. She reached up, putting her arms around his neck and he pulled her more firmly towards him. Betty Jean felt so good in his arms. So right, like she belonged there, like they were made to hold her. Carla flashed across his mind and he closed his eyes, squeezing Betty Jean tighter.

She'd been doing that lately. Carla. Jumping out at him when he least expected it. She leapt into his thoughts while he showered or when he made love to Betty Jean. Even when he was at work. It didn't matter when or where, she would just be there determined to have his attention.

After feeling Betty Jean's pain when he spent the weekend with Carla that last time, he'd broken it off. Well, not exactly. He hadn't been brave enough, strong enough, man enough to break things off with her in person or even over the phone. He'd simply stopped calling her and wouldn't return any of her calls. He ignored her calls during the day and turned off his phone when he got home every night. One day she left a message telling him he was full of shit and never called again.

That was a couple of months ago. And he didn't know which one of his heads, or if it was his heart, but something in him missed her. There was a piece of him that ached to call her, to hear her voice. Maybe just a quick *"You been okay?"* Or maybe they could meet for a drink or maybe they.... No. He gave himself a mental shake. He would not contact Carla. Maybe this business of moving to California would be a good thing. It would definitely put Carla out of his reach. Hopefully, remove her from his mind as well.

Six

She hoped she was wrong, but she wasn't. The stick in her hand only confirmed what she'd known for weeks. She was pregnant. Had the stick been able, it would have told her that she was also stupid. Very, very stupid. In fact, she was further into stupidity than she was into her gestation.

She did want a baby.

But not like this.

As she had already told herself, she was further into stupidity than she was into the pregnancy. The way things were currently going in her life, she just couldn't imagine trying to have a baby. They'd been careful. She could count on one hand the number of times they had unprotected sex or their protection had failed. She remembered his condom breaking once. *Only takes once*, she reminded herself, sick at heart. She stood in the bathroom closing her eyes for a long moment. When she opened them again the stick was still pink.

In disgust, she snapped it in half and threw it in the trash. She braced her hands against the sink seeking composure and losing. Tears stung her eyes, but she fought to keep from shedding them. Crying wasn't going to help her. At least she didn't have to worry about his reaction. He'd be happy. They'd talked about children, or at least he had, but so much was going on for her right now, the timing sucked. Her efforts in maintaining composure weren't enough and she slid to the bathroom floor. Wrapping her arms around her drawn up legs, she cried. Great big, soul felt tears.

Her stick had turned pink.

**

Entering the living room, Ezekiel smiled at Betty Jean's bowed head. She was sitting on the floor, surrounded by magazines. She was house hunting. "Find anything you like?" he asked, kissing her forehead. Stretching out on the thick carpet beside her, he picked up one of the books where she had pages marked. "Five bedroom, four baths? No three bedroom shack for you, huh, BJ?"

She blushed. "We have three bedrooms now and I love this place. So there!" She leaned over, kissing him.

"I guess you'll be able to afford any damn thing you want." He was glad for Betty Jean. She deserved to be on top and he was happy to see it happening. He was secure in himself and wasn't intimidated by her success. He picked up another book, pointing out a house that was reduced to three million dollars. "Let's get this one."

Betty Jean glanced at the book, saw the mini mansion he was pointing at and turned her head back to her own magazine without commenting. But the look on her face said enough.

"You *do* plan to be my sugar momma, don't you?" He looked at her from over his glasses.

“Of course,” Betty Jean smiled broadly, teasing, “and you can be my bitch.” She tried to jump up and run, but he was too quick. Laughing they rolled across her real estate magazines. When their rolling came to a stop, Ezekiel’s body covered hers.

“Why so big starting out? Why not something smaller and work up?”

She lifted her shoulders in a small shrug. “It’s not that much bigger than what we’re in and maybe Sheila will need a place until she finds something. I don’t know how much she has saved.”

“Nothing,” he interrupted. “What? I’ve met Sheila. Her nails, outfit, shoes and accessories always match. She’s always color coordinated and the height of fashion. Mostly name brand and not the cheap name brand either. The good kind. It’s obvious she’s broke.”

“Color coordination is nothing spectacular,” Betty Jean said, having no other defense for her assistant.

“True, but Sheila takes it to a whole different level. With her it has to be damned time consuming, not to mention expensive. That may be why she’s always late to work. She’s trying to change her nail polish or something.”

Betty Jean slapped his arm. “She has her nails done once a week, then coordinates her outfits to match the nail color. She’ll wear various shades of one color. Stop looking like that, you know what I mean, pink, rose, mauve. The same thing, but different. That way she can be sure her nails match her outfit. Sometimes she changes colors mid week, but rarely.”

“Okay, I take back the broke comment.” He rolled off her. “But I now add insane.”

“A talented coordinator, as she stated on her resume. Maybe she’ll help me decorate the house.”

“The five bedroom shack for poor people you were looking at or the reasonably priced home I picked out? Did you see how much it was reduced? You’ll be saving an easy three mil.”

She smiled more broadly. "Um-hmm."

"You know what'll happen if you let Sheila decorate, don't you?" He nuzzled her neck.

"We'll have five different shades of one color throughout the house?" She put her arms around his neck and he rubbed her backside.

"Nope." He kissed her lips. "You'll be broke and insane just like Sheila." Jumping up, he smacked her bottom, then raced up the stairs two at a time.

Betty Jean laughed. "I'm not going to chase you, boy!"

**

"What's wrong?"

"I haven't got a clue." He sat on the side of the bed. A light sheen of sweat covered his forehead and he felt queasy.

Betty Jean placed a cool hand against his head, saying, "You don't feel like you have a fever." She looked at him puzzled. "Do you want me to turn the fan on for you? You're sweating."

He wiped his forehead with a hand that trembled lightly and lay back in the bed, waiting for his illness to subside. Betty Jean adjusted the circulating fan until it was centered on Ezekiel. "Do you need me to get you something?"

Her concern was genuine.

For the past three mornings, Ezekiel woke with the same symptoms. He was clammy and nauseated. The nausea preceded a feeling of weakness that stayed with him until mid morning, before mysteriously disappearing. It was the third morning of his infirmity, so Betty Jean ruled out a twenty-four hour virus. He wasn't a woman, either, so she threw out morning sickness. She thought that he could have a touch of the stomach flu and suggested he visit a doctor, but he declined. He assured her he'd be fine and since he was no longer sweating, she allowed herself to be shooed out the door.

**

"Fill this out please. Put your real name on the form, but remember this number." The woman pointed to a number written in red ink at the top of the authorization form. "When we call you it will be by number, not your name, so please be attentive. We use numbers to protect your privacy."

Carla took the clipboard from the woman and was glad to see the pen that was chained to the metal clasp. She'd forgotten to put one in her purse when she left the house.

"There will be a fee for the sonogram that's separate from the cost of termination. Both fees must be paid for in advance. After determining how far along you are, you will be sent in to speak with a counselor."

Carla nodded her head in understanding.

"Do you have any questions?"

She had a few, but the receptionist's brisk tone and attitude prevented her from voicing them. What did her questions matter, anyway? The end result would still be the same. Finally, she shook her head in the negative.

"Please have a seat. When you've completed your form bring it back to me along with the sonogram payment. We take cash, money orders and credit cards. No checks, please." She slid the frosted window closed just as the last word cleared her lips.

**

Carla had just begun her shift and already she was tired and ready to go home.

She should be resting in bed, but she couldn't afford the luxury of a full week off. She'd only been able to take three days. It was her first day back at work and she was feeling every minute of it. She glanced at her watch again. Ten more minutes and she could take her break. Five more hours and she could go home. She plastered another smile on her face and greeted her next customer.

**

"You had a phone call while you were out."

"Who?"

"Who else?"

"My honey?" she used Sheila's favorite pet name.

"Nasty self. His name is Ezekiel."

Betty Jean laughed. She tried to stay alert and on her toes, but Sheila always managed to slip by her. No matter how Betty Jean would twist her response, Sheila always made her say something else. "Do I call him back?"

"Don't think so. He said he might be running a little late tonight, but nothing major. If you feel like waiting he'll cook."

**

"The cutest thing I've seen in a long time is at the front counter and he wants to see you."

Carla, who had just sat down for her break, looked up from the book of poetry she was reading. "Tell him to go away."

Monica stared at the younger woman like she had three heads. "One, you don't even know who it is. Two, he is too good looking to be sent away."

"Please, Monica, I don't really care who it is. Play secretary for me and say I'm not here."

She was shaking her head. "I already told him you were. He asked for you and I said 'Yeah, she's here. She just started her break. Let me get her for you' and now how am I supposed to go back out there and say you're not here? I should look the liar?"

"Please Monica."

"Oh, all right, fine, make me lie." The older woman turned to leave the small break area. "But I say it's a waste."

Carla was used to men she didn't know asking about her. Usually, it turned out to be a customer who thought she meant something hidden when she asked, "Would you like a little hot apple pie with that?" She was tired today and wasn't about to get up for nonsense. She had thirty minutes to rest her feet. Finding the poem she'd been reading, she reread it from the beginning with no intentions of getting up.

Monica came back into the break area, breathing hard with her ample chest heaving. "Spirited young buck, I'll give him that." She put a hand to her bosom, her face flushed. "I had to cuss him out, girl. I didn't want to lie and say you were gone. So, I told him you were busy perusing some paper work and couldn't come to the front."

Carla pulled her eyes away from the poetry her nose was buried in. "So," she hunched her shoulders in a small shrug, smiling, "you lied."

Monica pointed a finger dangerously at the open book. "Are you not perusing that paperwork, as we speak? Were you not too much of a little snot to get up and go up front?" A smile filled her eyes, softening her words.

Carla smiled. "I'm not worried about you, Monica." She turned back to her book, searching for the spot she left off on. She'd just purchased the collection of poetry and short stories and hadn't had a chance to read it thoroughly yet. She was passing the bookstore when it caught her eye in the window. *Too Deep For Tears.* She immediately empathized and went in to buy it. Now, if she could only get a chance to actually read it.

"He didn't believe me. He was very solicitous, until I said you were busy, then his eyes went all dark and he asked me, too politely if you want my opinion, to try again. But I said that unless I missed my guess, there were over one hundred pages that you had to go through and I wasn't going to waste the trip at my age and certainly not for a measly ten dollar bribe." Monica was well over fifty and that's all anyone knew about her age. She'd started working at the popular establishment part time to fight off boredom years ago.

Her husband was killed in a traffic accident involving a common commuter and as a result of the insurance settlement she received, Monica was an independently wealthy woman who didn't need to work. She just needed to be around people who did or at least that was the excuse she used for her continued employment.

She put on her uniform for the first time three years after burying her husband. Four sizes and two decades later, she still suited up for twenty hours a week. Always smiling. Always on time. She'd seen many of her coworkers come and go, but Monica enjoyed being around lively people and never considered leaving.

In the twenty plus years of her employment, Monica had never cashed a check. At least not for her personal use. When she'd first started working she'd become friendly with a fellow employee, a young woman who was trying to attend college but obstacles kept being thrown in her way. When Monica met the young woman she was already beginning to see those obstacles as insurmountable. Monica feared she would be like so many other females that let pregnancies that came too soon in their lives shape, guide and even, sometimes, ruin that life.

The young woman would swing from being very optimistic that she would be enrolled in school the coming semester to tragically depressed that she wouldn't. There was always a bill to pay. Something late, something due and she was the only parent providing for her infant son. It was the Friday that Monica was to receive her third check that she discovered what to do with them.

She'd entered the break area to find her friend mournfully surveying her check. "I can't do it, Monica," the girl said, sniffling. Monica walked over to her. Saying nothing she placed her hand on the girl's shoulder, encouraging her to speak further.

"It's not enough. Again. I want this so badly, you know, to be somebody." She lifted her shoulders in a sorrowful shrug, looking up at Monica with tears on her lashes. "I just want to be something more than what I am. I want to be somebody my son will be proud to call mommy. I don't want him to always think of hamburgers when he thinks of me." She'd spoken softly and Monica had to strain to hear her.

"I can't be a superwoman. I've tried. I can't do it. I want to go to school. I want a future that's worth having. But I'm stuck in this rat hole and can't afford to get out." Her voice was filled with a bitter sadness of acceptance.

"I don't think I've ever asked you what you want to major in," Monica said in the same hushed tone the younger woman was using. Which was good because she didn't trust her voice to go much higher without cracking and she'd end up on the bench next to her friend crying, too. And that wouldn't do anyone any good.

"Accounting. I wanted to be a CPA."

Monica's head snapped up. "I don't think I like the sound of wanted." She'd been deep in thought trying to find a way to help the woman without insulting her. Monica was well acquainted with the power of pride and knew how it could run a head and steer the heart.

The girl rose from the bench. She smashed her hat back on her head and squashed her check into her pants pocket. "What's it matter anymore, what I want? I have to be realistic. I just have too much going on right now. My son is still in day care and diapers. I have rent, a car note and that's not even mentioning the basics of just keeping the two of us alive." She was shaking her head while she was speaking, tidying her clothes in a distracted fashion. Her mind was on matters other than her appearance and her gaze was fixed on that. She was seeing nothing in the little break room but more defeat.

Monica had turned to her locker. Retrieving her purse she rummaged through the lipsticks, tissues and other debris until she located her checkbook. Nonchalantly she called over her shoulder, "How much is the semester going to cost?"

"That's the thing, Monica, it's not really even that much. I'd only be a part time student, because I'd still have to work. Two classes, that's only six hours. The fee is less than eight hundred dollars. Nothing. But it's too much. All I want is a chance and I can't even get it." She shook her head wearily, resigned to her fate. "I have to go before Derrius comes back here looking for me."

Monica replaced her purse. Closing her locker, she turned. Taking two steps she crossed the room and closed the door, leaning her back against it. She stood staring at the younger woman, mentally appraising her, until a brow was raised in question. "I've never done anything like this before so I don't know the proper protocol, but I dearly hope what I'm about to do will neither embarrass nor insult you because my intentions aren't to do either." When she stopped speaking, she reached for her friend's hand and placed two checks in it.

"What is this?" she asked, then realized that *this* was two checks totaling thirty-five hundred dollars. "Monica, I can't take — Where did you — Monica — Monica?" There was a confused rush of stammered words as she was shaking her head, looking at the checks in her hand incredulously.

"Well, the one is to pay for this semester with the part time schedule you want *or* combine the two and you can go to school full time and work part time, if you'd prefer."

"Yes, but —" The younger woman questioned, still shocked by the unexpected act of kindness.

"I can easily afford it. You aren't snatching any food from old Monica's mouth and you know I only work part time, don't you? I wouldn't mind keeping an eye on little Joshua when I'm not working and you wouldn't have to pay me either. I can use the company. That should help with your day care expenses, hun?" She smiled widely.

"Sugar, we can do this!" she said, hugging the speechless young girl who wept silently.

And so began the Amanda Fund.

Monica donated all her checks to the tuition fund she created. Each semester the Amanda Fund awarded one thousand dollar scholarships to six young women, for a total of twelve thousand dollars a year so twelve girls could attend college. The only requirement to apply for the award was motherhood. Monica said she chose mothers because it's harder trying to achieve your goals when you have other people to look after, as well.

That and, though she was never one herself, she knew how motherhood could change, delay or kill a dream. She was tired of seeing the light go out in so many women who had so much potential. College was a way of improving a life and since she had no children of her own, she *adopted* twelve each year and tried to give them what Amanda wanted, a chance.

She'd been after Carla for years, trying to make her one of her girls, to no avail. The first week Carla was on the job, Monica told her about the scholarship program. She'd tried bargaining, telling Carla she wouldn't have to apply for the program. She'd be one of the twelve automatically, but Carla only said she'd think about it.

Each semester Monica made the same offer and each semester Carla's response was the same. *"I'll think about it."* But Monica could be really stubborn. She didn't know if Carla ever really considered her words, but she knew each semester, she'd recite them anyway. Monica was determined to see Carla achieve. She knew intelligence lurked beneath the tough exterior and she saw no reason why it should go to waste.

Carla smiled, shifting in her seat. "He offered *you* a bribe?"

"Sure did. Ten whole dollars just to get you to come to the front. I asked him if I looked like a pimp, if my paper hat was velvet." Monica's eyes twinkled merrily. "Once he understood that I'm not above making a scene, he left, but he wasn't too pleased about it. I'm certain he'll be back, though. He looks like the type."

"The Come-Back type?" Carla asked, grinning with sarcasm.

"The *I'm Too Damned Good Looking To Be Turned Away* type."

Again, Carla laughed. "He'll adjust." She turned back to her poem, dismissing the admirer from her mind. She recited softly:

sometimes the one we love, is not the one we need
inadvertently, they bring to our lives such grief
the strong arms that held us
become the ties that bind
and the love is only 'lovely'
when we view it in our mind
the things that were so dear
become so far and out of reach
and we learn the hurting lessons
that only life can teach
love isn't always enough
to keep two hearts together
and maybe eternity just wasn't our 'forever'

The poem was one of her favorites in the collection. It made her think of Thomas when she first read it and she wondered about their *forever. How long would it be? Or were they over, lost in the past somewhere? Was their forever already played out, gone for good in just a few years? Or was their forever merely on hold and they would eventually find their way back to one another?* She sighed heavily, unable to answer any of her questions, and turned the page in her book.

Seven

She could hear a baby crying. The infant's wailing was what woke her. She left her bed to soothe the child, but couldn't find it. She tried to follow the sound of the crying, but it seemed to come from so many directions. The child's torment enveloped and eluded her all at once. Running from room to room, she searched the countless rooms in an endless corridor, but still couldn't locate the babe.

The crying intensified. The uncomforted anguish grew louder until she covered her ears. She was afraid the sound would never leave her mind, but still she sought the child. Finally, her search completed, she found nothing. The house was free of infants. She was alone, but still the baby cried. Its piercing scream filled the air, choking her until she could scarcely breathe.

He shook her again, harder. "Carla, goddamnit! What's wrong with you? Wake up!"

Carla opened her eyes to see Thomas's worried face leaning over her. She stared at him with wide confused eyes, unaware of the tears that wet her face. Thomas brushed the blond bangs from her eyes. "You okay?"

She was in the middle of a bad dream when he came in and it looked like Carla was on the losing end of it. It had taken some time for him to wake her and even now, she looked as if it still held her.

"Baby?" There was concern in the question.

Carla shoved back the blanket on the bed and slid over, saying nothing, only watching Thomas's face silently.

"Are you serious? You want old Thom to lie in your bed?" He asked the question lightly, but they both knew her action carried great weight. Thomas had not been invited to Carla's bed since that night he'd lost his mind and struck her.

His eyes met Carla's, but she didn't speak. She lay in the bed just as she had moments before. The fear and confusion were gone from her eyes, but sadness replaced them. Sadness and something else that Thomas couldn't fathom, but it helped decide him on the matter and he questioned his luck no further. He sat on the side of the bed removing his Timberland boots, before sliding his baggy jeans off.

Carla watched him undressing silently. It had been a long time since she wanted Thomas to touch her, but just then she couldn't think of anybody else she'd rather have holding her. She wanted to hide, to lose herself in the curve of his arm like she once did. She wanted to feel his arms around her and know that she was safe and someone loved her, because despite his banishment into exile, she knew Thomas loved her.

When he was clad only in his A-Frame tee shirt and boxer shorts, he climbed into the bed. He'd barely settled himself against the pillows before pulling Carla to his chest. She was lying pressed up against his side with her head on his chest listening to his heart beat. Its beat seemed fast even to her untrained ear, but its pace always quickened when he held her. She was glad that she could still affect him so and a ghost of a smile touched her lips before fading into her lingering sorrow.

Thomas lifted the golden strands of hair that lay across Carla's back and he, too, smiled. He never knew what the hell she was going to look like when he came over, but the end result was certain and the same. She was going to look damn good. Even now with the phantom of the dream still holding her, she looked good. Delicate and vulnerable.

He couldn't believe he was lying in bed with his arms circling Carla. He still couldn't believe how he fucked their relationship up. Carla was his. She always had been, but he'd let some hater shit, a fabrication someone made up, set him off and he'd lost her. He'd let his so-called boy's bullshit, a bottle of E & J and his already fucked-up temper allow him to put his hands on Carla, his own heart. After that night, she was never his again.

She still let him come around for their shorty's sake, but everything else between the two of them was dead. They did a lot of things with Ebony as her parents. The three of them spent a great deal of time together, but only because of his little Ebony doll.

Carla never willingly let him touch her.

He might sneak in a hug or a squeeze here and there when he just couldn't resist the way she looked, but nothing like this. Curl herself around him and let the hands that hurt her, hold her? Never. But here he was and he could scarcely credit his good fortune.

"Why are you crying, Carla?" He asked the question softly, rubbing circles on her back. He closed his eyes in contentment. She felt so damned good lying next to him.

She didn't answer.

"I've always loved you, girl," he said, filling the silence.

If she wanted to act like she wasn't soaking the front of his tee shirt, fine, but he'd been holding in his own feelings for a long time. Too long. He planned to take his chance and say his peace. He was tired of acting like his heart wasn't bleeding behind losing her. Tonight he wanted to be real.

"I don't know if I've ever said I'm sorry. I mean aside from just that night, I don't know if I ever made you understand just how badly that shit I did touched me. I ain't saying it's about me, Carla. I just mean I don't know if I ever told you how bad I felt about what I did to you. What I did to us and our little shorty. Our family. I don't know if sorry is enough. I mean even to my own ears when I'm thinking about how I fucked up, I'll think how I'm sorry and it don't ever sound like it's enough. I guess it's like my momma be telling my old man all the time, *sorry is a sorry word.* It don't change shit." His arms tightened around Carla's body. He lay there wishing with his whole heart that the word could move mountains and turn back time, stopping the senseless action that made its usage a necessity. *Had he never struck her....*

"I haven't held you in two years, but that's not the reason I'm lying in this bed with you. Well, not the only reason, because you know I like having you in my arms," he added sheepishly. He paused then, not knowing what he intended to say. He wanted to tell her two years' worth of stuff. The things he'd lain in bed and thought about all night. The words that would sound perfect in the dark, but ridiculous in the light of day.

He'd loved Carla forever, since they first met. He'd never wanted anybody else. And in the two years he hadn't had Carla, he hadn't had anybody else, either, including E & J. He'd definitely put that shit behind him. He'd done a lot of things to punish himself since he lost her, but not having other women wasn't one of the punishments or at least he didn't see it that way. He hadn't made a conscious decision to stop seeing other women; he simply hadn't wanted to be with anyone else.

He wasn't one of those men who needed pussy to exist. He could take it or leave it.

He didn't really look at the other negative things he'd done away with as a punishment anymore, either. He'd seen his crew for what they really were after that madness with Carla and he cut them loose, each and every one of them. He used to think it was their jealousy that cost him Carla, but now he understood it was his own fault for believing them and responding the way he had. The way they had intended. He'd been flying solo ever since, but it was cool. He got into less trouble by himself.

He felt better nowadays, too. His system was clean of all the shit he'd been putting in it. The liquor, cigarettes, weed. The occasional prescription pill minus the prescription. The women were easy to let go of too. None of them measured up to his queen and it didn't make no sense letting one woman live in the shadow of another. Anybody he hooked up with would be behind Carla. No doubt.

Carla was the mother of his child, of his little Ebony doll, and she was also the only girl he ever truly cut for. Even aside from his little shorty, it was just her, Carla, the one he loved and wanted. He could have had someone to take home with him. He was not bad looking with his smooth mahogany skin and dark eyes. He wore his hair cut low and faded. It had deep waves that looked nearly blue in their blackness. Since he dropped all his habits, Thomas discovered that he liked working out. He ran and lifted weights regularly. Rest assured, he could have taken home nearly any woman he wanted, but he hadn't. That wasn't what he wanted. He didn't want a woman under him or a woman he could have for the night. He wanted Carla. His Carla.

He wanted her to look at him again the way she once did. He needed her to love him again. He wanted to beg and plead his case, but he didn't know how to do that either. In fact, his head didn't know how to capture and form into words any of the feelings that were swirling around inside his heart. He could feel moisture at the corners of his own eyes and quickly wiped it away. He pulled her to him and kissed the top of her head, settling for, "I love you, Carla. I'm sorry you ever hurt because of me and I hate that I ever made you cry. I should be the last person causing you to shed tears." Thomas shook his head slightly. "Especially, knowing all I know."

In the darkness, the words sounded wholly inadequate to his ears. It was like he hadn't said nearly enough and *nothing* right or worth saying. He was certain her ears had heard the same. Thomas closed his eyes. He rested his head against his upraised arm and the pillows that were propped behind him. "Hell, Carla, I wanted to be the one who protected you from that kind of madness. I wanted to protect you from everything." He paused briefly, adding in a near whisper, "You should never have needed to be protected from me." Not trusting the thickness in his voice, Thomas fell silent, listening to the quiet that embraced the apartment.

He felt Carla drift off to sleep again some time later, her demons apparently subdued. He reached to pull the comforter more securely around her shoulders, recalling her habit of burrowing into the blankets. He didn't know what could have frightened her so badly that she'd want him to hold her, but he'd play hero all night if need be. He'd be her defender against all things, both real and imagined, and he'd get it right this time.

**

Ezekiel was distracted again.

He was separated and held apart from her in a place she was having more and more difficulty reaching, as of late. If she was honest with herself, she'd admit she was also losing the desire to reach it. She wasn't certain if it was their impending move halfway across the country that was resting so heavily upon his mind, seizing his thoughts and pulling him away from her, or something else entirely. Something a bit more sinister. Something like Carla Jeffries.

Sometimes Betty Jean imagined that she felt Carla's presence, alive and warm, sitting with them at a table, or when they went to the movies. Sometimes even in their bed, Carla would be there in Ezekiel's kiss or it could be as she said, she'd only imagine Carla's presence. The woman was in her mind alone, not Ezekiel's.

It was so this evening. She was imagining things.

They'd gone out for Thai, but Ezekiel, who merely pushed the food around on his plate, seemed to only occupy the chair across from her. His mind was somewhere else and Betty Jean could just imagine with whom. She hated that after so much time had passed, she still couldn't shake her insecurities about Carla. She couldn't stand feeling insecure about anything, but everything Ezekiel did was becoming about Carla. If he was pensive. *Carla.* Deep in thought. *Carla.* Not in the mood to make love to her. *Carla.* Ignoring the shit out of her over dinner. *Definitely, Carla.*

Betty Jean frowned into her glass of lemon water and the spicy food on her plate was forgotten. It was disturbing just how much she thought of Carla or thought of Ezekiel thinking of Carla. She was tired of the entire situation and increasingly looking forward to their move west. If the idea of moving wasn't bringing peace to Ezekiel's mind, it was doing a world of good for hers. Soon she'd be able to put the whole sorry mess of Carla behind her. She'd know true serenity at last, which brought to mind the upcoming weekend. "Would you like to come away with me this weekend?" The question shook Ezekiel from his thoughts and he raised an eyebrow in inquiry.

Betty Jean smiled beautifully as he at last joined her at the table, his attention restored.

**

"And you're certain you don't want to tag along? A four and a half day weekend, which will make next week a four day work week, as well." Betty Jean added the last part in a coaxing sing-song voice for the countless time as she made a third turn around her office. She wanted to make certain she wasn't leaving some small detail hanging loose that would unravel into a huge mess before her return on Tuesday morning.

Stepping before her, Sheila placed her hands on Betty Jean's shoulders, bringing a halt to the frenzied circling. Betty Jean was always like this before leaving the office unattended for any period of time.

"Sweetie, your man is going with you this weekend. He will be with you this afternoon when you leave and later on your final trip. You guys will wine, dine, dance, look at real estate and have a blast together, but girl, none of my men are coming with me. I'm going to have to start a whole new harem on the West Coast and that takes energy. I'm going to need to stock up before we leave." She smiled mischievously at Betty Jean, wiggling her brows suggestively.

"Maybe film some shit before I go. I may need something to tide me over during the lean days of rebuilding. Can't find a partner? Pop in a tape, I always say. No telling how long I'll have to entertain myself, but in the meantime, it's Spencer, *hung like a horse*, fine ass's weekend. And he's into some wicked shit that's worth filming." She shook her head at Betty Jean in mock insult. "Hell no, I don't want to go with you and your man this weekend!" She laughed, lightening her words.

Removing her hands from Betty Jean's shoulders, she brought them to rest on slender hips that were draped in lime green silk, green being the color of the week. Her eyes held Betty Jean's for a moment, searching for something she couldn't quite put her finger on in her friend's demeanor. Something she wasn't certain she liked.

"You all right, honey? You look like, I don't know," she paused, shrugging. Searching for a description of her friend's countenance, "You certain about," a brief hesitation as she chose her words carefully, "this *move?*"

There was a strange emphasis on the word that left a reasonable doubt in Betty Jean's already frazzled mind as to whether the move to California was what she was really being asked about.

Betty Jean frowned slightly at the inferred question. What could Sheila be thinking? What was she really asking and why? Of course she was certain about the move, her new job, her man and her Carla-free life, for damn sure. She didn't hesitate to inform her assistant of her thoughts.

Well, not all of them.

Carla was her own secret torment, her cross to bear alone. It was one thing to know yourself a fool and quite all together something else to broadcast the fact to anyone who was willing to listen. As much as she'd love to unburden herself and get everything off her chest, her hurt, her fears, her humiliation, she wouldn't be able to look Sheila in the face again if she did. Sheila would think Betty Jean a fool. No, she would not confide her secrets to anyone. She'd be too ashamed.

She was this educated, no nonsense kind of woman ready to take the universe by storm. A *Grab Life By The Balls And Give Him A Big Ole Squeeze* kind of gal, to quote one of her daddy's favorite sayings. She was supposed to have it all together and basically, she did.

Except for Ezekiel.

Ezekiel brought her to her knees time and time again. She only told Sheila that he was her light, her strength. Her lips would not betray the knowledge that he was also the cause for most of her pain. That he was responsible for some of her darkest moments. She could never admit that, though he provided her with so much strength, Ezekiel Johnson was also her greatest weakness.

Too many times Betty Jean could recall shaking her head, tsking or telling one of her girlfriends to simply walk away from her man. And his crimes were far less heinous than any she'd given Ezekiel a full pardon for. These days her head remained still, and in one place on her shoulders, and her lips were silenced from all tsking or friendly advice. She couldn't tell others to grab a broom and sweep, when her own front porch needed a good dusting. She'd be damned if she'd shine a light on her own stupidity by confessing her problems to somebody.

Satisfied that she was picking up only on Betty Jean's regular anxieties before a trip and nothing else, Sheila relaxed her radar. Picking up Betty Jean's monogrammed briefcase from where it lay on the office couch, Sheila headed for the door. She grabbed her friend's arm as she passed. "Come on, you. The office will not fall apart or fade to black or anything else climatic because you're missing a couple of days." Sheila shot Betty Jean a look over her shoulder, a smile tugging at her lips. "Hell, who'd care if it did, girl? Not us. Our hearts are in San Francisco, baby!"

Setting her worries aside, Betty Jean laughed at Sheila's version of the popular Tony Bennett song and allowed herself to be pulled from the office. She still had half a billion things to do before their flight. All week, she'd known she was leaving too much to be done last minute, but it couldn't be helped. Especially not her trip to see Mr. Grailton, who was having one of his customary panic attacks about his account. He demanded to have a copy of his portfolio in his hand by the end of the day, saying something along the lines of perishing on the spot without it. Insane. Pure and simple. The man had a problem that really did require psychiatric counseling. She'd bet cash money he had at least five copies of the thing already. He just wanted attention.

Not wanting to hear him complain about how impersonal delivery services were, she'd *volunteered* to hand deliver the document herself. The last time she'd sent a delivery service he took to his bed for two days, refusing to sign any paperwork, stating that he wasn't certain if he wanted to continue doing business with such an aloof firm.

Insanity at its worst.

Mr. Grailton was a decent enough guy, if a bit eccentric. On any visit, if you could get in and get out without him talking your ear off about everything under the sun, you were doing pretty good. She could spare him five, ten minutes tops. Then, aloof or not, she had to go. She and Ezekiel were on a pretty tight schedule with not enough room to spare for spur of the moment detours. Exactly what her dropping off the portfolio in person created. A spur of the moment detour that was keeping her from doing one of the other zillion things she needed to do before their flight, fully aware that the number kept increasing.

**

"He said to tell you, he'll wait."

To this Carla raised an eyebrow in inquiry. She reached for her soda, using it to help her swallow the huge bite of cheeseburger she'd just taken. Covering her mouth, she asked, "Who the hell is he?"

Monica shrugged in response. "Obviously someone with time on his hands, because he said he'd wait. And I got the impression he was thinking *however long it takes.*"

"Too damned much time on his hands, evidently," Carla grumbled before rising from the bench, taking another bite of her burger half way up. *Damn, she was hungry.* She leaned forward so the ketchup sliding from between the buns landed with a soft plop on her tray and not the floor. Tendrils of black hair had come loose from her pony tail and she used the back of her hand to wipe them from where they curled across her cheek. She picked up a French fry, smothered it with ketchup, shook her head and regained her seat.

She spoke around the small bit of potato. "Tell him I'll be out in ten minutes. I am not rushing myself, leaving my food or throwing it out cold later. Whoever the hell he is, he'll have to wait if he wants to talk to me that badly."

Monica turned from the break room smiling. "I didn't think your little greedy behind was going to leave your food. You weren't fooling nobody."

"You saw me stand up!" Carla defended herself, taking another bite of her burger.

Without bothering to turn around, Monica laughed. "All for show. That's why I said you weren't fooling nobody."

Twenty-three minutes later Carla, having finished her lunch, plus two sundaes, returned to the front counter where Monica handed her a bottle of cleaning solution and two towels.

"What the hell is this for? I'm not going into the lobby." Carla frowned at the cleaner, deeply insulted. The restaurant had people assigned to keep the lobby and bathrooms clean and she wasn't one of them. Bad enough she had to work in a grease trap, she had to draw that line at cleaning it.

Monica guided her towards the swinging doors that lead to the lobby. "I'm the ghost of Christmas future. I'm trying to show you what you have to look forward to if you keep refusing to attend college."

Carla, who was allowing herself to be propelled forward, stopped, digging in her heels. "What?"

Monica smiled at her confusion. "See what I mean? He's on the side lobby, dumb ass." With a final shove she pushed Carla through the swinging doors. "A person with an education would have known something was up without it being drawn out for them, *See Spot run* style."

"A person with common sense would have just told me to go to the side lobby, too," Carla called over her shoulder before turning the corner, where she came to an abrupt stop. The side lobby was empty. Carla hunched her shoulders, assuming that her guest had grown impatient after all and left. She hunched them again dismissing the visitor from her mind. She stood in the lobby for a second debating her options.

Cleaning tables went a little bit against the grain, but she was on the side lobby with two towels in her hand and it *did* need attention. Having decided to do her good deed for the day, she sprayed four tables with the cleaning solution. She was just finishing wiping off the third table when the door to the men's room opened and Ezekiel stepped out.

They were both caught off guard by the other's presence, not expecting that only the thin wood of the door stood between them. Not being as surprised by her appearance as she was by his, Ezekiel was the first to recover. He took in the uniform pants that fit her nicely. Today she wore a black and powder blue polo style shirt. Her hair was a single black pony tail that hung to the middle to her back. Her nails had been done with a French manicure. He always liked that. French manicures were classy. Of course, Carla had to make her stand out and instead of the tips being white, they matched the blue of her shirt. Damn, she looked good and he told her so.

Having recovered from the shock of seeing him, but still at a loss for words, Carla stood staring at him as if she were made from stone, but her mind was a chaotic jumble of thoughts. She should just walk away. Pick up her towels and walk away. But he looked just as delicious as ever. Unconsciously, Carla licked her lips. She ran her tongue across the lip gloss she wore, making it shine with even more invitation than before. It was not an act of desire. Her mouth had just gone dry when she looked at Ezekiel and she needed to loosen things up to speak.

Her lips looked wet, giving the impression they'd just been sucked on or needed to be badly. The errant thought caused Ezekiel to swallow visibly. His own throat had gone suddenly dry.

Carla bent to hastily wipe the last remaining table.

Damn, but she didn't want to talk to him.

She'd put him behind her. *He was sucked out with everything else*, she thought. She just wanted to be left alone. Aside from speaking to him, Carla found that she didn't even want to look at Ezekiel. She wished he weren't standing before her. Gathering her supplies, she made ready to leave. Zeke's hand on her arm stopped her.

She stood frozen by the touch and stared down at the offending appendage until he removed it from her person with a whispered, "Sorry," weakly he added, "I didn't want you to leave just yet."

"Just yet? Did you have further use of me, Ezekiel?" His name was not the soft caress that he remembered but he guessed he couldn't be choosy. At least she called him by his name, and not out of it, like the last time he'd heard her voice. She'd been right, too. He was a stupid son of a bitch. He shouldn't be there, but there he was. He hadn't done right by Carla, but Betty Jean was – He pushed the thought from his mind.

Betty Jean would keep for a while. Right now, he needed to straighten things out with Carla. He could tell that she had him on thin ice with a warm front on the horizon. It was also plain that he didn't have much time before the ice broke and he'd be toppled into the freezing water. Drowning. From the way she was looking at him, or more specifically, by the way she was avoiding looking at him, he could tell that she would not throw him a lifeline if he did fall. He would go under and she'd walk away unconcerned.

Even standing there now in her presence he felt like his head was barely above water. He could scarcely breathe and was afraid of trying for fear that she would turn and leave. He would love to simply stand and stare at her bowed head. He missed her more than he'd realized.

Carla wanted to raise her head. She truly did, but the coward in her was firmly in control and refused to do anything as reckless as looking Ezekiel Johnson full in the face when he stood so close. She wanted to desperately, but she was just beginning to heal; to move past him and his bullshit.

For just a second, Carla could hear the faint distant cries of an unborn child and she turned her head sharply to one side in an attempt to dislodge the sound. There was no baby. Again, Carla gave her head an abbreviated shake. She did not need this shit. She could feel tears tugging at the back of her eyes and fought madly to keep them there, to hold them in check. She wasn't wasting anymore tears on this particular tragedy, especially not in front of any witnesses.

She called upon every deity she could think of who might help in her hour of need. She wasn't picky, either. Anyone would do. Any angel with some free time. *Anybody* who could save her from Ezekiel. From herself and her stupid decisions. She looked around, but no avenging angel swooped in to help. It was up to her. She made to move past him, but he stepped to the side with her.

After a maddening half waltz, Carla stood still. Apparently, her prayers had been heard. Someone was still on her side, because she felt anger replace the tears in her eyes and her head snapped up in confrontation. Her eyes fastened on Ezekiel, who was observing her quietly. Knowing his time was running out rapidly and wanting to speak before she turned and did the same, he said the first thing that came to mind.

"What the fuck do you want?"

"I have a plane to catch."

The sentence collided with the question and they both frowned with puzzlement and in Carla's case, agitation.

"What?"

"What?"

Again, their words occupied the same space at the same time. Carla held up her hand, stopping Ezekiel's flow of words that kept bumping into her own. "Why are you here, Ezekiel? Are you just now returning my calls? Did you lose your cell phone and you just remembered where I work? You came by my house lots of times, but I was never in?" she asked sarcastically.

Before he could open his mouth in response, she shook her head. "No. It doesn't matter. Spare me whatever the fuck you were about to say and just leave." She tried to push past him but to no avail, he stood firm and solid. "Or let me leave. Just go, damn! Buy a goddamn hamburger or something if you must be in this building, but leave me alone and let me get by."

He ignored her outburst, saying, "I wanted to talk to you, make sure you're okay." He hunched his shoulders feebly, letting his voice trail off. "I was worried."

Carla folded her arms across her chest, raising an eyebrow at his words. "Worried? About me? Why now? You haven't been concerned about me. I didn't warrant any of your concern when you stopped answering my calls. When you were so deeply moved with concern for Betty Jean that you left me out in the fucking cold with no jacket, no sweater, you didn't even leave me an ear muff. I was just left out there, stuck the fuck out and it's been what, two, three months since then?"

She nodded her head, up and down, considering the length of time that had passed. "Wow! Your great concern let you wait nearly ninety days. A quarter of a year passed before you could come by and put your soul at ease."

She turned her head to the side. Her dark ponytail swished across her back. “Poor thing. However did you make it?” Her face was a mask of imitated concern, before turning to granite. “Man, I’m fucking freezing.” She alluded back to her earlier comments and rubbed at her arms for warmth.

“Hell, I’m frozen solid. Dead.” Her eyes held his unwavering. All traces of sadness and indecision were gone.

Ezekiel tried to hold her gaze, but couldn’t.

He became very focused on his shoes. He shoved his hands deep into his pockets and hunched his shoulders again. “I have a plane to catch.” He didn’t know why he repeated the words, but they sprung from his lips without conscious forethought. Even his subconscious mind knew he shouldn’t be there. It thrust his impending trip with Betty Jean forward and just as resolutely, he pushed it away.

He had time. Granted, not as much as he had when he’d first come in, before waiting for Carla to finish her lunch. He had at least ten to fifteen minutes before he had to leave. He would be pushing it a bit, but he’d make it. He just needed to get things straight with Carla first.

“I’ve never been to the airport, so I have no clue how to get there from here. I do know it’s on the other side of town, so you’d better hustle if your flight’s leaving soon. Are directions all you needed?”

“I do need directions, but not the route to the airport. I need you to tell me how to fix this.” He removed his hands from his pockets, spreading his arms wide to encompass their entire situation. “How do I fix this, Carla?”

She folded her arms more firmly across her chest. “I thought you did fix it, Ezekiel. Wasn’t that the purpose of pushing me out into the cold and leaving me there these past few months? To fix a problem with your beloved Betty Jean, whose tender feelings needed comforting? You did fix it, remember? You pulled up your pants and turned your back on me, on us, on our —" She shook her head, catching herself before speaking the word.

She held her hand up, palm out. A stop sign; she didn't want him to pass. Carla closed her eyes again, blocking Ezekiel from her eyesight, if not her heart. Damn him for showing up. Damn him for making her want to tell him her secret. Their secret. She damned him a third time, before going on. "Never mind. None of this matters anymore. It's too late."

He felt an unexpected stab in his heart at her words. Too late. It was not as though he hadn't tried to see her before now, because he had. It wasn't his fault that she'd been out in the cold freezing, as she put it, for months. He had tried to check on her. His timing always sucked. Just as it had today.

Whenever he'd come by it was either her off day or she'd been on break or there'd be some other reason that he couldn't get to her. Hell, he even tried to bribe one of her coworkers once to go get her from the back, but that hadn't worked either. At first, he'd taken the difficulty of reaching her as a sign that perhaps he didn't need to get in touch with her at all, but he'd ignored that thought for too long for it to suddenly have an impact on his decisions now.

He tried to explain all this to Carla. He listed the times he'd come by her job or called her, only to hang up when she answered. He wanted to talk. He just hadn't known what to say. While he explained all this, Carla, who remained stony-faced, merely lifted an eyebrow at his more extravagant attempts. Angry with her apparent nonchalance, Ezekiel turned his back to her, running an agitated hand down his face. Turning back to her, he stared at her a moment before speaking. "I came before now, Carla. That's what I'm trying to tell you, and I didn't wait a quarter of a year to do it, either. I first came a while back and they said you were on vacation."

Her brow rose higher at the thought of going on vacation. Her? Not likely. And a genie was going to pay her bills?

Reading her look, Ezekiel frowned. "Well, fuck, Carla. I don't know where you were. They said you took off and wouldn't be back till the end of the week." Maybe it was the hurt he was experiencing that caused him to add, "Funny, how once I was gone your rent wasn't such a worry for you anymore, hun?"

She didn't know what the fuck he was implying, but she recognized the tone and responded to it. "Fuck you and whatever your twisted little mind has thought up." She stopped mid sentence, realization dawning on her, tightening her features. She threw one of the wet towels at him. The towel hit him in the face before landing on the tiled floor with a barely audible plop.

"Fuck you. Fuck you, Ezekiel." Her look raked him from head to toe. Her eyes moved up and down his body as each syllable dropped. She curled her lip contemptuously, saying, "You think I put a price tag on my pussy just because you left me, you bitch?" She hissed the question as tears sprang to her eyes.

"Not that it's any of your goddamned business, but I traded days, moved shit around, begged, borrowed and pleaded to get those fucking days off. Days I needed to take and it wasn't a week. I was only gone three days!" She held up three French manicured fingers that shook slightly with her anger as she pummeled the air with them. "I hustled and busted my ass to still be able to pay my rent on time and handle my shit on a short check."

"I'm just saying, that's all. The last time we were together I wanted you to take a day off and you wouldn't. You started complaining about bills you had to pay. Then as soon as I'm gone, there you go, taking off. Maybe the next nig —" He broke off, shaking his head.

"Maybe the next nigga, what? Paid my rent? Kept my lights on? Paid me to stay home and fuck all day, like any good prostitute?"

"I never called you a prostitute."

She went on, cutting off his interruption. "Yeah, you called me a fucking prostitute. You called me one every time you touched me then went home to your gal. I was just too stupid to get paid for my services. I can't believe this shit, I really can't. *I'm* the one who got the raw end. *I'm* the one who lost my —" She shook her head at the injustice unfolding before her as anger bubbled to the surface again, unchecked.

"I'm selling pussy, because I missed three days from work." Incredulously she shook her head at the ridiculous irony of her situation. "I did what I had to do. Both times. First with my schedule and then —" She stopped again. Taking a deep breath, she choked back more tears, barely whispering now. "Don't come here after I — After —" She paused, unable to get the words past her lips and waved a hand in the air, as if it could fan her pain away. It couldn't but she felt more fortified when she said finally, "Don't come here stepping to me like that after every fucking thing I've been through. Just go away. It can't be that hard for you to leave me." She tried to push past him, but he caught her in his arms, pulling her to him.

"What happened, Carla?"

"Do you care, Ezekiel?" She asked the question sincerely, with tears in her eyes. She hunched her shoulders, looking at him. "I don't want to waste your time with something you won't even care about."

Ezekiel stared at Carla's face. He could see in her expression that something had happened since the last time they spoke and he was anxious to know what it was. It couldn't have been good. She was too hurt about it. Maybe her busted ass baby's daddy did something to her, he thought. He could never get her to see ole boy wasn't any fucking good; now he probably did something to her himself that proved Zeke's warnings correct.

He squeezed Carla gently, urging her to speak. "What happened, Carla?"

"We had a — I had our —" She squeezed her eyes shut, the words catching in her throat. She could see herself at the clinic being strapped down and warned not to move. She tried again, her voice still a paper thin whisper. "I had our baby scraped from my womb."

She could have said it less graphically, but she figured if she had to experience it, he could bear the telling of it. If she sounded graphic and extreme it was because her actions had been graphic and extreme. No one had held her hand or tried to soften the blow for her; she would offer no such courtesies either.

Ezekiel held her in shocked silence, his arms tightening in response to her words. He didn't know if they tightened to hold her more securely or to stop his heart from falling out and onto the floor. His child. She'd said, his child had been scraped from her womb. He'd given her his seed and she'd aborted it. Threw it away like refuse, but still his arms circled her, holding her to him, ceasing her struggles. He wrapped one arm firmly around her. His hand spanned her waist until his long fingers touched the side of her stomach. He used his other hand to cradle her head, pressing it against his chest.

Carla pushed against him, struggling to find control of her feelings. Then she felt Ezekiel's fingers moving feather light against her stomach where he held her and arms that pushed, began to pull. She crushed herself to him, holding him tightly, crying for what she'd lost. For what she'd given up.

He said nothing.

What could he say? Shit. He shook his head, mute. What the fuck could he say? He'd been a father. For how long? He'd had a shorty. A fleeting smile pulled at his full lips, as a tear slid from beneath his rimless frames, ignored.

Ezekiel took a deep breath, pulling Carla closer. *I'm sorry, Carla*, his mind formed the words, but they failed to cross his lips. He was sorry. Sorry. His being sorry wouldn't change any damned thing. His child would still have been sucked from the security of its mother's womb. Poor Carla, to have gone through such an ordeal alone.

"Did you —" He stopped, considering his words carefully. "Did you already know you were pregnant when we —" Again his voice trailed off.

She shook her head against his shirt front, understanding what he was asking. Did she know she carried his child, while they were still together? "No. I didn't find out until later. After I stopped calling."

"Why didn't y—" He stopped himself from asking the question. Why didn't she call, he was going to ask, but call him for what, when he was too much of an asshole to even speak to her? But still, his heart argued, with something so important at stake, she could have called and said something. She called and left that fucked up message. Why couldn't she call and tell him about his child? Unless, of course, his wasn't the number she needed to dial.

Hell, with the way she let ole boy run up in her space all the time, maybe she hadn't called him for a reason. Then, too, his aching heart whispered, maybe there hadn't even been a baby. After all, he had nothing but her word to go by. Women made up shit like this all the time just to be hateful.

Carla could feel the shifting emotions racing through his body just as surely as if he had spoken them aloud. She pushed away from him, sniffling. Her eyes were red from crying. "Fuck off, Ezekiel!"

He raised both his hands in front of him as if to ward her off, palms out. "No wait, Carla. I know the baby was mine. Everything just sort of caught me off guard and I'm tripping, that's all. You know how I feel about having a baby. This shit is fucking me up some."

"Yeah, well, it wasn't a fucking picnic for me either. Look, Zeke, I need to go back to work." She spat out the first excuse that came to mind, trying to escape his presence. He was not willing to let her go so easily.

"No one's come in since we've been standing here." He indicated the mirror that ran the length of the building, allowing them an unobstructed view of the front lobby and serving area. "Can we talk, Carla?" He looked down at her bowed head, wanting to pull her to him again and hold her. "Please, Carla, I've missed you."

Carla lifted her gaze to Ezekiel's face. He was so damned good looking it was ridiculous. If there was no law about a man being too handsome for his own good, or the good of others, for that matter, there should be. Carla looked into his face and recalled the day they met. She was in the mall shopping with her daughter when he approached her.

"This is going to sound like a line, but you are very sexy. Not just your face either, or your body," then he smiled that killer smile of his, adding, "but the total package. Man!" He looked at her in such an appreciative way that she laughed. He was so obviously full of shit.

Now, she tried to smile, but failed. "Go, Ezekiel. You have a plane to catch and we both have other stuff to do." She moved past him. This time he made no effort to stop her. He'd stretched his fifteen minutes to spare all the way into thirty-five minutes. All he had time to do was race home and pray he hit all green lights in route. Picking up Betty Jean's laundry from the cleaners was out. He'd never make it to the cleaners, then to the house in time. He'd think of something to tell Betty Jean.

He shook his head trying to clear it. He didn't know how he was going to think up anything worth a damn to say, when all he could focus on was his child. His unborn child who would remain that way.

He fumbled with the keys in his pocket feeling suddenly alone. Heavy sadness seized him. He left the building with his head hanging low and a tiny weight in his heart.

Eight

Betty Jean looked out the window to the scenery that was zipping past and let out an audible breath. *Bless his heart*, she thought, they were going to make it to the airport in time.

Catching another flight wouldn't have been a big deal, but she was glad it hadn't come to that. She didn't want to get into California too late in the evening to enjoy it. She liked to drop her things at the hotel, then go out and explore. She always thought that arriving somewhere in the dead of night was a waste of a good opportunity. Half the fun of traveling was seeing the city and being able to compare it to all the other places you've seen. At least it was for her and now, thanks to the taxi driver's lead foot, her arrival wouldn't be ruined. She'd been to California before, of course, but it was a long time ago.

As the vehicle pulled to a stop in the passenger drop off zone, she glanced at her watch. It was 2:30. They'd made it with no time to spare. She knew the flight was on time, because she'd called the airport just before the taxi arrived at the house.

When they announced the flight to San Francisco, she was ready to board. Everything she needed for her three-day trip was packed carefully in the carryon bag she had slung over her shoulder. She hated waiting at the baggage claim area and had learned a long time ago how to travel light.

The attendant was smiling when she extended her hand for Betty Jean's ticket. She was a young woman of medium build who looked professional in her navy blue uniform with her brown hair pulled back away from her face and secured with a dark scarf. She glanced down reading the ticket then looked up sharply at Betty Jean. Her smile faded.

Seeing the smile retreat, Betty Jean looked at the ticket in the woman's hand and was surprised to see Ezekiel Johnson's name staring back at her. Oh, crud, Betty Jean thought; smiling brightly, she reached into her purse. Feeling her hand close around the object she sought, she pulled it out, offering it to the attendant in exchange for the first ticket.

"I'm sorry. I didn't know I still had that."

"Perfectly all right," the attendant chimed as she waved Betty Jean through.

She'd told herself to leave the ticket at the house just in case he showed up, then she thought it best to bring it along, in case he intercepted her at the airport. But in the end, the speedy arrival of the impatient taxi driver and her harried departure from the house sealed the ticket's fate and she'd forgotten to take it out of her purse.

Betty Jean's shoulders seemed to lift of their own accord in a dismissive shrug. She didn't know what the hell was wrong with Ezekiel lately. He was still distant with her and the strain was beginning to take its toll. Maybe this weekend without Zeke will be just what I need, she thought, determined to be strong.

She was settled into her seat, staring out the window to the fading runway, long before she realized there were tears on her face.

**

Carla wrapped the satin robe around her slender form, tying the sash with more force than was required. She cursed under her breath at the knock at the front door. It was late, she'd just gotten home and wasn't in the mood for company.

She clenched the cigarillo between her teeth, freeing her hands to unlock the door. "I'm right here, goddamnit!" she hissed as the knock sounded again. Pulling the chain across the wooden frame, she secured the door before opening it an inch. When she saw who was standing on her porch, she shook her head. "Shit."

He raised an eyebrow. "Damn. It's not that bad, huh, Carla?"

She made to close the door, but he put his hand against it, stopping the action. He shook his head in warning. "I don't want to make a scene, but that won't stop me from kicking in the door to talk to you."

She stared one-eyed at him through the crack in the door allowed by the chain. With a roll of the eye she pushed the door forward slightly, so she could remove the chain. When the door was free she stepped aside. Ezekiel came into the living room, seating himself in one of the chairs that faced the television set. He waved a hand back and forth beneath his nose frowning. "That shit stinks."

"Number one, I wasn't expecting or desiring company. Two, the smell doesn't bother me at all. Three, it's my fucking apartment and four, get the fuck out if you don't like it." She held the door for a moment, allowing him time to consider, in or out.

He continued to sit, so she closed and locked the door, assuming he meant to stay.

"I was about to get into the tub, Ezekiel. What do you want?" She perched herself on the arm of the couch, diagonal from the chairs. She pulled strongly on the marijuana. She knew Ezekiel hated it when she smoked, even more than Thomas did. Usually, she wouldn't smoke in his presence, but she no longer felt that she owed him anything, including common courtesy, and demonstrated this by blowing a long stream of thick smoke into the space between them.

"I thought you had a plane to catch. Did you need directions after all?" she asked into his continued silence.

He shook his head slowly at her question. Addressing her statement, he said, "Yeah, I think I missed it." His chin was nearly on his chest, which was so unlike the Zeke she knew, a small part of Carla began to unthaw, however reluctantly.

"So, why are you here, Zeke?" She could hear the faint trace of concern in her voice and frowned in irritation. He looked so unlike himself, so lost that she felt something pulling her towards him just assuredly as if she'd risen from her perch on the couch and crossed over to him. Torn between the unexpected worry that something was really wrong with Ezekiel and the anger that she would even give a shit if it were, she sucked her teeth in impatience. Placing her short into the ashtray on the table, Carla stood. "I'm getting into the tub if you aren't going to say anything."

Ezekiel grabbed her hand, tugging her towards him. She lost her balance, landing in his lap, her legs over the arm of his chair. Momentarily stunned by the suddenness of the action, Carla was slow in reacting, which gave him a chance to get his arms around her waist before she could rise. Feebly, she pushed at his chest with her open hands, but his hold was strong and he didn't seem inclined to loosen it. She stopped struggling with a resigned sigh.

Again, Carla's mind demanded to know what had brought Ezekiel to her apartment, but she knew him well enough to know that he wouldn't open his mouth unless or until he felt like it, so she remained silent. Shifting, she tried to reach the ashtray, but couldn't. She felt his hold tighten when she stretched for it. She knew he wouldn't relax his grip enough for her to grab it, which irritated her more, seeing as it was her house, her lungs, and no one had asked him to come over in the first place.

High-handed men always got on her nerves and Ezekiel Johnson's hand was one of the highest out there. She'd just seen so many other things in Zeke she liked that she allowed him certain liberties from time to time, but that was then. They weren't screwing around anymore so she didn't have to put up with his mess. She was bracing herself to rise, by any means necessary if it came to that. She was getting off his lap and relighting her smoke. If she had to, she'd – He spoke then, cutting into her thoughts of rising. The softness of his words took all the wind from her mounting anger.

"Do you know —"

Carla tensed, waiting for him to complete his question, to clarify his meaning. Did she know what? Several heartbeats passed in silence before he spoke again. His voice was just as soft as before. "Do you know if our baby was a boy or a girl? Or was it too soon to tell?"

Carla closed her eyes against the sharp stab of pain she felt and nodded her head slowly. Her voice was whisper soft, as well. "I know it was a girl. I mean, they didn't say it or anything. It was too soon to tell, but I know it was a girl." Ebony's face swam across her vision and she brushed away tears. What if Ebony would have ended in a pan on some doctor's office floor? She saw again her legs spread apart and strapped down. She heard the sucking noise of the equipment and bolted up from Ezekiel's lap. Her emotions gave her the necessary strength.

She grabbed the short from the ashtray, relit and inhaled in one fluid motion.

"Baby girl," she bit out. "I didn't ask. I didn't want to know. I didn't want to make it that real for me, you know, what I was doing. It's one thing to be able to live with the knowledge of what I did to my own child, but to know I had a baby boy or another sweet little girl —" She shook her head, scratching her forehead with her thumbnail. "No, that would have been too much. But I know it was a girl. I can feel it." She touched a hand to her chest looking off into a distance only she could see. "Could feel it, I mean," she corrected herself, shaking her head. Carla turned and walked from the living room. When she returned she held a folded sheet of paper out to Ezekiel.

He took it from her hand. Unfolding it, he sat motionless, staring at the would-be face of his child. The sonogram picture showed him nothing but a mass of darkness, but he saw what was hidden in the photo. He saw his child, his son maybe. He couldn't make out anything he could understand, but he knew what was there and so stared at the photograph. His imagination filled in the gaps until he could visualize his child as vividly as if he were holding him in his arms.

At the time, she didn't know why she had demanded to have the sonogram photo. In fact, she was rude in getting it. The nurse she'd requested it from had raised an eyebrow and said how unusual the request was, coming from a mother about to terminate her pregnancy.

"*Unusual or not, I paid sixty dollars for that picture and I want it. It's mine.*"

They'd been on the verge of refusing to perform the procedure. The nurse she'd spoken with had already strongly advised additional counseling *before she made a permanent decision,* but the doctor okayed her request. When she left the clinic, they had what was her child and she had the only picture it would ever take. Watching his bowed head and the slight way his hands shook, she knew why she'd wanted the picture so badly. It was his. Nothing much, but some tangible proof of what they had shared.

Nine

When she opened her eyes, light was flooding in from the two windows above the bed. She lay perfectly still not wanting to disturb the peaceful tranquility of the morning. *The morning*, her mind echoed the words and she closed her eyes again, sighing. She snuggled deeper into the blankets. She could not remember the last time she felt so....

A hand closed around her breast before curving around to her back and she abandoned her thoughts. The hand slid down the slope of her smooth back, resting momentarily in the deep hollow at the base of her spine. The hand began to stroke back and forth. It traveled from her back, across the swell of her behind, to the firm flat of the back of her thigh, then retraced its path.

Feeling warm lips pressed gently to her shoulder, she sighed again, but this was a different sound, pulled from a far deeper source of contentment. While her first sigh had been induced by sleep and a strong desire to stay that way, the second was a powerful mixture of sexual gratification and a gluttonous yearning for more.

At the same moment she felt the butter soft kiss on her butt cheek, she felt hands turning her over to lie on her back.

He kissed the flat of her stomach, sucking briefly at her navel. His hands spread her legs until he lay between them. He planted his face in the v of her thighs, then licked her with long, deliberate strokes, teasing her flesh.

She moaned, deep in her throat. She slid her legs up the sheets until her feet were flat on the mattress with her toes curling into the tangled bedding; her fingers went into his hair.

He'd knelt before her last night, but then he'd taken his time. The slow sensuous lick of his tongue remained slow and steady until finally she'd found her release. This morning his tongue quickened its pace, sending hot liquid fire through her body. She could feel herself building, reaching. Her body was demanding release. Then he stopped.

She opened her eyes in a frustrated question. Her body was quivering on the brink of Heaven and he loomed above her, smiling. Damn, he was handsome. *Sexy as sin*, her mind supplied. He also was without a condom, she thought, reading the inquiry in his eyes. He was poised between her thighs with his erection pointed straight at her. She shook her head in the negative. There would be no free falling. No condom, no sex. Period.

White teeth flashed before he dipped his head to nip at her breast. "I only had two and I used both last night," he said, by way of an explanation. He tongued the other breast, attempting to coerce her.

"Well, it looks like you're going to the store if you plan to finish what you started." She reclined back on the pillow, only slightly disappointed. She did wish, though, that he would have said something before he got her mired in anticipation.

He glanced at the clock on the night stand and experienced his own jolt of disappointment as he shook his head. "There isn't enough time for me to go to the store, come back and do this right." He kissed her stomach. "And still get to where I need to be on time."

Oh, well, she thought, but refrained from saying it. Instead she slid from beneath him and rose from the bed. "Do you need to shower before you leave?"

He collapsed on the bed when she rolled away from beneath him and he looked at her now, his face half buried in the pillow. "Am I being thrown out?" He sat up as he asked the question and began looking around for his boxer shorts.

"It's getting late and I need to get to work," she called from over her shoulder as she left the room. Moments later he heard Ashanti's voice filling the outer room.

He also heard the other voice, strong and true, blending with that on the radio, overriding it. She hit the notes and held them effortlessly. In his opinion, she held them even better than the voice coming from the stereo speakers, but then he could be biased.

She was standing in front of the stereo, her back towards him in the doorway. When he finished dressing, he called out, causing her to turn. "You have a nice voice."

She ducked her head shyly. Ignoring the compliment, because she didn't know how to respond to it, she walked over to the door and opened it. He crossed the room and his hand closed around hers on the knob, large and warm. The things his hands had done to her flashed through her mind and she looked away from them.

"Am I going to see you again later?"

She shook her head slowly, looking into his eyes. "No."

He was bending his head for a kiss when her reply jerked him back to look into her face. She was still shaking her head. "No, I don't want your phone number and I won't give you mine. I really appreciated last night and I enjoyed your company more than I can tell you. It was really nice, but I can't do this. I told you about my situation last night and it hasn't changed in these last few hours. I was attracted to you and for reasons I'd rather not explain, I gave in to a desire I would have normally ignored or not felt at all. I needed to be held last night," she said shrugging.

"I needed to feel desired and wanted and so many other things that I can't begin to tell you. You provided those things and we shared an experience, but it can't be more than that." She offered a timid smile. A simple uplifting at the corners of her mouth, a lip shrug, but it failed to soften her words or the look in her eyes which held none of the warmth of the previous evening, only a foolish resignation to accept what had to be. A plea that he would accept, too.

He stared at her a moment longer, willing her to bend, to change her mind. This was a first for him and he wasn't certain of how to proceed. Should he just leave and let it go at that or should he play by his own rules and pursue her? He liked the way she looked, even all disheveled from sleep. He didn't know what luck had brought her into his club last night, but he was thankful for it. He only wished he had a chance to get to know her better, but it was obvious by the way she was ushering him out the door that she wasn't too interested in the possibility.

He bowed his head to her before stepping through the door. "It was my pleasure to meet you and pass the evening with you," he said formally. Then he was gone. He didn't think his parting words had been too clever, but what else could be said when you meet a gorgeous lady, have a wonderful night with her, wake up curled around her, only to be thrown out, no strings attached?

He pressed the button for the elevator, glancing over his shoulder at the room down the hall, feeling disappointment wash over him with a crushing weight. Aside from the fact that they were sexually compatible and just thinking about her made him tingle with desire, he liked talking to her. She was interesting and he would have loved the opportunity to explore a relationship with her further.

**

Betty Jean lifted one soap-covered hand from the whirlpool tub and adjusted the temperature of the circulating water. Steam curled up from the bald patches of space left behind by the drifting bubbles. It was early, but she'd ordered champagne and strawberries from room service. Her usual breakfast when she stayed in a hotel. It made her feel pampered, like one of the privileged. Besides, it was her weekend to indulge and she planned to go at it with full gusto.

Last night's escapade came to mind and she blushed. Glad that no one was around to see the color on her cheeks, she sank below the surface of the water. She was lying with her back flat against the bottom of the tub and held her breath. Her hair floated around and above her, giving her the look of a ghostly sea spirit. An angel drowned.

When she felt like her lungs would burst if she didn't, she allowed her head to break the surface of bubbles. Suds slid down her face in small rivulets that she wiped away. Oh, she was no angel. Even if she had been one before, last night would surely have gotten her kicked from the kingdom.

It started out perfectly normal with no insidious plans to do wrong.

She had an uneventful flight, where she'd managed to get a lot of thinking done, but nothing untoward. She'd spent most of the flight trying to conquer her emotional state which shifted from concern for Ezekiel's safety, to being hurt that he missed the flight and hadn't bothered to call or contact her in any way, until finally she reached anger having concluded that nothing had happened to Ezekiel. If he had been in an accident, she would have known. If he was running late with the intention of being on the flight with her, he would have called. He had simply blown her off. Even feeling that was the true cause for his absence, her only planned form of retribution was to have a damned good time without him.

Still, *nothing lurid in mind.*

She'd tried to call him at the house once she'd checked in to her suite, but there was no answer and she refused to call his cell phone. Her gut told her that Ezekiel was all right. Again, she thought that she would have been contacted if anything serious was wrong, something life threatening. She would have felt it in her heart, but something *was* wrong. She was in California by herself, and paranoid or not, Betty Jean just knew it had something to do with Carla.

She hadn't come all the way to the West Coast to sit in her room and sulk, so Betty Jean showered and changed to go out and greet California. She wore black hipsters that accentuated her figure and flared slightly at the bottom with a drapery peasant blouse. The blouse had long sleeves that hugged her upper arms tightly, then fanned out, draping loosely from her elbow to the middle of her palm. She completed the look with black ankle boots and was ready to absorb a little of San Francisco.

Instead of hailing a cab, she decided to remain on foot and see what was surrounding the hotel. She was so out of sorts at the airport that she took a cab to her hotel instead of renting a car. Without Zeke, she didn't want to take the chance of driving around a strange city and getting lost. She was lucky though, because there was plenty to be had on the long avenue. She was walking past different establishments, trying to decide where to eat, when she ended up at Rufio's.

One moment she was walking past the club, marveling at the line that was already pretty lengthy given the earliness of the hour, and in the next, she was part of the growing line that snaked the building like a serpent.

"Is this place always like this?" She leaned forward, speaking to the two women in front of her.

"Girl, yes. That's why we got here so early tonight. The last time we tried, we couldn't get in at all." The woman speaking rolled her eyes dramatically. "We stood in line a long time, too."

"But it's not so bad tonight because it's Thursday and it's not ten o'clock yet," her friend chimed in, bouncing to the music flooding out from the club. "Is it your first time at Rufio's or should I ask, is it your first time trying to get in to Rufio's? Because it is not the same thing."

"For real. You can be here all night and not get through the doors."

Betty Jean craned her neck to see what was happening at the front of the line. "I just arrived in town a little while ago, actually. I'm staying at the hotel down the street." She jerked her head to the left and behind her. "I was actually on my way to get something to eat, but then I saw a line and jumped in it," she said, smiling widely. "My mother was right. Apparently, I will jump off a roof because everyone else is doing it."

The two other women laughed having heard similar comments growing up. The second woman to speak held out her hand. "Ariel, and this is Tamara. Welcome to the state of the surf and the sun. Why are you in town?" She spoke rapidly, barely leaving space between her comments and her friend elbowed her.

"Ignore her, she's nosy as hell by nature. She —"

"Shhhh," Ariel broke in. "He's walking the line again."

"What's that mean?" Betty Jean asked, half expecting to see God, because of the momentary hush that came over those waiting to be chosen. "I saw him doing that earlier." Betty Jean turned to look along with everyone else in the line, waiting to see who among them would be deemed worthy enough to enter his kingdom.

"Girl, it's up to that fine, long, tall drink of water right there, who gets in and who doesn't. He walks the line and selects people. If you aren't selected, chances are you won't get in. So sorry," she said, waving bye-bye with her fingers.

Tamara shook her head at her girlfriend's slight exaggeration. "That's not exactly true. You can get in without being picked by Mount High," she said, indicating the man making his way slowly down the line. "They just always have a crush at this place. Everyone wants to be at Rufio's. So, to keep the crowd under fire code, they monitor who gets in and when. Besides, who wants to be all smashed up and crowded? But if you get here early enough, before the crowd gets too thick, you can just pay and go in."

"It's just nearly impossible to get here before the crowd gets too thick," Ariel added, stretching to see where the line walker had gone.

"Once it gets a little too crowded they're more selective about who gets inside, but it's understandable. It's good business sense," Tamara said, watching as two men and a strikingly beautiful woman were led to the front of the line. As they entered the building, the line walker turned and began his hunt again. "See? Good marketing. Everyone wants to be selected. And with prime meat like that inside —" she said, referring to the three that had just gone in. "The selection process is one of the reasons this place is so hot. It's been the spot for years when all others crash and burn after a few months of popularity. It's cool to find out the next day who got in and who hung outside all night hoping."

"Are you serious? That's —"

"Shhhh," Ariel broke in, again, cutting off Betty Jean's protest. "Here he comes!"

Betty Jean was just wondering if she even wanted to get inside, when the man walking the line stopped in front of her. He'd taken one look at her, smiled, grabbed her hand and tried to pull her away from the line. She'd resisted his tugging, insisting that her "girlfriends" got in, too. Only when he offered his elbow to the other two women did she let herself be pulled forward. She noticed more than one catty look thrown their way, but she didn't care.

They were at Rufio's and they were going in.

Byron hadn't stopped when they reached the door as he had done with the other patrons. He told one of the three men standing sentry at the doors to continue scouting the line and had gone inside with the three of them. He remained by Betty Jean's side most of the night. He got them a prime table and made sure their drinks stayed fresh. Ariel and Tamara had loved it. When Ariel exclaimed that no one was going to believe they not only got into Rufio's by selection, but received the VIP treatment as well, Byron signaled for the club photographer. The five of them took at least twenty pictures together. One of them was of Betty Jean and Byron, but she left it in the ladies room just before leaving the club.

All night Byron made sure to include all three women whenever he did something chivalrous, but it was obvious that Betty Jean was his true focus.

When she said she was leaving to get something to eat a few hours later, he offered to escort her. One on one, they were able to talk more freely and she'd told him about Ezekiel. Not their whole life story, just the basics. That they lived together and had been a couple for years. She told him they were having their problems, but every relationship did, so it was nothing to cause concern. She told Byron about her promotion and new job and that she was in California for the next few days house hunting. She told him that Ezekiel was supposed to come with her, but had missed their flight.

She'd been attracted to Byron at first sight. It would have been hard not to be. He was handsome, intelligent, had a great sense of humor and his body told of a man that liked being fit. He should have been gracing magazine covers and she told him so, but the compliment made him blush and shake his head. Apparently, he'd tried that field of work and hadn't liked it much. The limelight wasn't for him. She pointed out that he was still in the limelight walking the line at Rufio's, but again he shook his head at her. He explained the differences in what he did then and what he did now. Before he was the pampered one, the center of attention. Now he got to make other people feel pampered and fussed over. Betty Jean laughed, having to admit, she did enjoy the way it felt being selected from a whole line of potentials.

The spot where they'd chosen to eat had a thin crowd, because of the hour, and after two hours of conversation, it was nearly deserted when Byron tipped the piano player to let him play while the gentleman took his break. When he sat at the piano and began to play, his attractiveness increased by tenfold. He said he'd been playing the piano for as long as he could remember and had thought about a career as a concert pianist, but changed his mind. It was a shame too, Betty Jean thought, because the piano keys had come to life under his touch. And so did you, she mused, adding more water to the tub.

Byron proved to be very interesting, indeed. Along with his looks and ability at the ivories, he was also fluent in three different languages, which during the night, as he loved her, he alternated between. Vaguely she could recall some of what he said. He knew French, Spanish and English. Some of the phrases he said she understood and what she didn't he translated for her in exquisite detail. She may not have fully understood the words, but she knew the sentiment.

He was also extremely well read and could quote great literary works and Bible passages alike. She knew he was probably showing off, but it was still impressive.

But even with all this, Betty Jean had not planned to sleep with him. She couldn't actually recall how they'd gotten from point A to B to him sliding into home base, but somehow during their conversation, she'd put Ezekiel out of her mind. She'd given Byron her full and immediate attention and ran with it. All she could say for certain was that she'd made a conscious choice. When he brought her back to her hotel, she had not needed him to walk with her to her room. Even if she had, it was already late, she certainly had not needed to invite him in; especially, feeling the way she was feeling. Sorry for herself because of Ezekiel, mad as hell at him and in the company of a man too damned spectacular to be real.

But he was real and it had been really late and she hadn't had to invite him in, but she had. And they had and it was a done deal now. She could dig at it and explore it and try to figure out why it happened or she could just say she met someone she liked and let it go at that.

It was like she said to Byron earlier, she understood how Ezekiel could have sex with other people. Sex was nothing. Prostitutes did it all the time. But what he did was more like living a double life. Ezekiel didn't simply have sex with these women, then move on. He wanted to keep them. He tried to give too many women too much and in the end, what each had was too little to satisfy any damned body. Sex was nothing, she repeated. Even if she hadn't already known that, last night would definitely prove it. Byron was the first man she'd been with, the only one in fact, since she met Ezekiel years ago.

She sighed. It was never that she thought she was above cheating, it was just never necessary. Ezekiel had always given her what she needed, but what she needed now seemed to be beyond his reach. Hell, it eluded her as well, because she sure as shit didn't know what she wanted, much less needed. She didn't know what would fill the hole that was growing bigger inside her. As she demonstrated last night, Ezekiel was not the only man she could catch. He wasn't the only man who wanted her and found her attractive. He was just the only man *she* wanted. She always said that anything you had to sneak around and do in the dark, wasn't worth doing. Now she begged to differ, because sex with Byron last night had definitely been worth doing.

But as good as it had been, there was still a part of her he hadn't been able to touch, because Ezekiel held it. Good or bad intentions aside, all she'd given Byron was last night and her body. Her tomorrows and her heart belonged to someone else. There would be no long term sneaking about, lies, deceit, mistrust or any of the other things that went along with living a double life. She was not an Ezekiel Johnson.

She sat in the tub considering her situation. While she didn't regret what she'd done with Byron, she did feel slightly dishonest. She'd betrayed a trust. Well, she told herself as she soaped up the towel to begin bathing, had Ezekiel not been fucking around and missed their flight or had he not been hurting her so badly, treating her with such carelessness, she would not have given into another's charms. An old Aretha Franklin tune came to mind; she hummed the lyrics softly:

Take me to heart and I'll always love
and nobody, can make me do wrong
take me for granted, leaving love unshown
makes willpower weak and temptation strong

She was startled by a knock at the door and her humming stopped abruptly. She'd put the Do Not Disturb sign out when room service left. Betty Jean had just made the decision to ignore the knocking, when the pounding came again. Sighing, she stepped from the tub.

"I'm coming, just a second!" She was wrapping the thick terry-cloth robe around her body, hurrying to cross the suite when the knocking came again. She reached the door and pulled it open with attitude. "I said I was —" Her voice trailed off into stunned silence.

Ezekiel smiled at the look on her face and kissed her forehead. "Yeah, I know. You were cumming. That's why I kept knocking. I didn't want you to cum without me."

Betty Jean stood dazed by his presence and so wonderfully thankful that she'd had the foresight to have maid service change the linens and clean the room before she got into the tub. There was no trace of Byron left in the room.

Lies and deceit, her mind echoed from her earlier thoughts as Ezekiel brushed past her into her room. *Lies and deceit.*

Ten

He expected surprise, but not the stunned silence Betty Jean greeted him with at the door and said as much. Betty Jean collected herself. Her mind was adjusting to Ezekiel's presence and her heart no longer threatened to leap from her chest. "Of course, I'm glad to see you. I didn't think you were going to make it."

Ezekiel looked at Betty Jean for a long moment, studying her face for any untruths. True, she said she was glad to see him, but she looked funny; it was as though she wasn't too excited about it. He tried to shrug off his feelings of speculation. He finally concluded she was probably happy he showed up, but still mad that he missed their flight. He crossed the space between them, intending to put his arms around her and apologize, but she stepped away, saying over her shoulder as she walked towards the bathroom, "You're just in time, too. I set up a few appointments to look at houses." She tried to keep her voice even as she reached for the towel on the sink. With her head buried within its folds, she rubbed her hair vigorously.

Her heart rate may have slowed since she first opened the door, but her equilibrium was still off. She kept thinking that if Ezekiel had shown up an hour or two earlier, he would have walked in on her and Byron. *Lord, Lord*, she thought, *how do people pull off this shit*? She came out from beneath the towel, letting it lay across her shoulders as she searched the counter for her comb.

Zeke stood in the bathroom doorway with his shoulder pressed against the wooden frame, his legs crossed at the ankles. "I didn't think I'd make it here before you left knowing how you like to get started early." The feeling that something wasn't right returned.

Standing in the doorway watching Betty Jean, he felt he was living in a What's Wrong With This Picture cartoon. Watching her wipe the counter clean for the third time and rearrange the various bottles of products she was using for her hair, he thought he figured out at least one thing wrong and asked, "Why aren't you looking at me?"

"I'm straightening the counter area, because I can't find my comb and I'm trying to hurry, so we can go." Her eyes met his briefly in the mirror, before dropping back down to her own reflection. "It's nothing personal, sweetie."

Without saying anything, Ezekiel reached in front of her. Picking the comb up from the counter, he held it out. Betty Jean took the comb and began pulling it through her hair, rolling her eyes. "I swear I didn't see that thing. You know how my hair is. This could take all day. This mess never wants to cooperate, especially when it's wet."

"Why'd you wash it? You already know what it's going to act like."

Betty Jean recalled the vivid images of herself and Byron that made her dunk her head beneath the water, oblivious to her hair, and shook her head. "It was not intentional, believe me. It just felt so good." Did her voice sound too pleasure-filled? It was rather sensual to her own hearing and she tried to make amends. Clearing her throat, she clarified her comment. "You know, lying in the tub. In the hot water," she added weakly.

She was mad, he thought. She sounded like she was forcing herself to talk to him. She didn't even ask him why he missed their flight. If was as if it were no big deal or she didn't care and that wasn't like Betty Jean. She had to be mad at him. It would explain her bizarre behavior.

He felt guilty. He knew how much she liked to enjoy her first night in a new place and because of him, she probably spent the entire night in her hotel suite. He'd tried to make their flight, but he was in such bad shape after Carla's news that he couldn't think straight. He wanted to go home to Betty Jean, but he wasn't up for conversation. He would have told it all. Every sorry detail would have been laid at her feet. He needed to be comforted and he always brought his hurts and pains to her, but yesterday he couldn't.

He'd driven around, circling the freeway instead. When he'd finally got his mind cleared enough to go to the house, she was already gone. He didn't blame her for leaving. They had a flight to catch. But by the time he'd made it home, he really needed her. He hadn't wanted to sit in a house that was suddenly too quiet, so he went back to Carla's.

He hadn't been able to unburden himself there, though, because he found he couldn't speak. He had no words to express what he was feeling. He was hurt and disappointed that his child's life had been aborted. He felt guilty for forcing Carla to make such a decision on her own. He never should have put either one of them in such a predicament where she felt a choice had to be made.

Then there was Betty Jean.

If she found out, he would lose her for sure. There had been so many emotions vying for his attention, that he'd spent the majority of the evening on Carla's couch staring at the only picture of his child he'd ever have.

Carla hadn't pressed him for anything. She tried to get him to talk to her when he first got there, but she gave up when she noticed his lack of enthusiasm and left him alone until he was ready to leave. It was after midnight before he headed home.

Now he was in California with Betty Jean, but it wasn't what he'd expected. He couldn't put his finger on it, but something was off. He stared at Betty Jean silently, watching her at her toiletries. The silence between them hung heavy in the air. He tried again for conversation. "Have you had breakfast yet? Maybe we can get something while we're out."

"Sure. Sounds fine." Her voice was a monotone.

Shit, he needed to clear the air. She was giving him the silent treatment. Betty Jean only did that when she was truly pissed off at him. "Are you still upset with me, BJ?"

She stopped brushing her hair to look at him. "Upset? What makes you think I'm upset with you or anyone else for that matter?"

Ezekiel hunched his shoulders. "You just don't seem like yourself. You slept late, which you never do unless you couldn't sleep the night before and the only time you have trouble sleeping is when you're upset."

He inclined his head towards the wine and strawberries she'd had room service deliver. "Drinking your breakfast? That's not like you."

Since she was certain she'd told him the story behind her wine and strawberries breakfast before, she didn't feel the need to go into it again. They'd stayed overnight in a hotel before and she always ordered the same thing. His ass was actually looking for a fight, she thought. She had to give him credit for having balls, if nothing else. He misses their flight, then shows up the next morning asking questions to piss her off.

She smiled a little. If he wanted to make innuendoes and play games, she could imply shit, too. "You know me, Ezekiel. When I'm upset I'm more prone to do something I wouldn't normally do." Saying that, she moved past him into the room. She laid a pair of low rise Levi's on the bed and dug around in her bag for a shirt.

Ezekiel watched her as she lotioned and dressed. He still couldn't shake the feeling that something was wrong, but he could tell that whatever it was, if anything at all, she didn't plan on telling it to him.

Betty Jean could feel his eyes on her, but didn't care. He was probably waiting for her to ask him what happened to him yesterday, but he could wait until the cows came home and she wouldn't give him the satisfaction of asking. He wasn't going to get a chance to use whatever lie he thought up. She stood to pull on her black thong panties, turning her back to Ezekiel's watchful eyes.

**

Though the morning had gotten off to a rocky start, the rest of the day went along smoothly enough. They'd looked at four houses, one of which Betty Jean really liked. It was a four bedroom home with both formals, an upstairs game room, hardwood floors, an island kitchen and a very dramatic entrance done in Italian marble. The house had beautiful landscaping and sat on five acres of land. For a moment, Ezekiel was afraid he wouldn't be able to get Betty Jean to leave it. He was certain it would be the house they chose and knew it when Betty Jean gleefully told the realtor to start the paperwork. After house hunting they'd had lunch at a nearby Bistro and had done some light shopping like any good tourist. All in all, they'd had a good day.

The sun was setting on the West Coast, bringing a slight temperature drop that begged for a sweater. It was a nice change from the smothering heat of the South. They'd just gotten back to the hotel to change for dinner and a night on the town when they were stopped by the desk clerk.

"Ms. Carlson, you've got a message," the clerk's voice called when he saw them. Betty Jean had inquired a number of times the previous day about messages when she'd been waiting to hear from Ezekiel, so the clerk who was slightly enchanted with her wanted to be certain she received the card that had been left at the desk. She walked over to the front desk and he handed it to her.

Betty Jean's brow was creased in a frown, not understanding. Who would be trying to get in touch with her? When she'd taken the card from the clerk she noticed there was writing on its back. She turned the card over to read the neatly sprawled note. *In case you reconsider*, it read.

Aware that two sets of eyes were watching her, the desk clerk's and Ezekiel's, she dismissed the significance of the card with a shrug of her shoulders. Sliding it into her back pocket, she smiled at the desk clerk. "Thank you."

They stood waiting for the elevator and that same nagging feeling that something was wrong returned to Zeke, not that it had gone far at any point during the day, and he asked about the card. He wasn't sure why, but he had the feeling that whoever left the card wasn't thinking about business at the time. "Don't tell me a realtor tracked you down already?" He said the words lightly, in a joking manner, to hide his suspicions. He doubted that the card was from a realtor, but it was the only thing he could think of without asking straight out who'd sent it. Betty Jean had never given him cause to doubt her, but something was up. Maybe some knucklehead had seen her last night, alone, and was trying to move in.

If so, he could forget it. Betty Jean was sewn up tight. Then again, he thought, she still had the card. If it had been from an unwanted suitor, she would have thrown it in the trash or torn it up. She hadn't done either of those things *and* she had yet to explain it to him. Or answer his question, for that matter. He was just thinking to ask her again, when her head jerked up and she looked at him. "What?" Ezekiel's voice jarred her from last night's memories. She wasn't certain what he'd said, but was sure some time had passed since the words had left his mouth and she tried to fill the silent air that hung between them. "I wonder if there's a good place to get Chinese around here. That would be good, but we'll probably be hungry again before the end of the night and need room service later," she joked as they stepped onto the elevator.

They were both silent in the elevator, each submerged in their own inner drama. She couldn't believe Byron left his card after what she'd said. Especially since he'd had to come back to leave it. Had he left it previously the clerk would have given her the message when she and Ezekiel first left to go out. What was wrong with him anyway? Most men would have jumped at what she'd offered. A great night, with absolutely no strings attached. Apparently, Byron wasn't like most men, because she had his card in her back pocket. A string. He'd even written his home number above the numbers already provided on the card. Damn, she thought, temptation was a terrible thing.

Ezekiel could see the play of emotions crossing Betty Jean's face and he didn't like it. Something was definitely going on and he was getting tired of feeling like the odd man out. Something was happening that he wasn't going to fucking like. He could feel it and he hated waiting for it. He sucked the inside of his bottom lip, grabbing the soft flesh with his teeth in an effort to remain silent, but it wasn't working. Suddenly he was filled with anger and wasn't quite certain where it came from, but it was there and building rapidly. They'd barely made it into her suite when he exploded. "What the fuck is going on, Betty Jean?"

She turned to look at him, surprised by his temper. "What are you talking about?"

"Right now, I don't goddamned know. I'm pissed off and I haven't any idea why, but I've got a feeling you do, BJ. You know exactly what I'm tripping off of even if I'm still in the dark. You've been acting funny since I got here and now you have mysterious messages waiting on you and shit. Who left that card for you?"

Betty Jean stared at him a moment. Again she was taken back by his tone and attitude. She felt her own temper rising and did nothing to stop it. "Who are you talking to like that? Me?" He merely held her look. His expression asked, who else? "Whatever, Ezekiel." She made to move around him, but he stepped in her path.

"Let me see that card ole boy just gave you."

She looked into his face, reading his eyes, then shook her head. "The message was for Ms. Carlson not Mr. Johnson. No." She made to move past him, but again he blocked her path.

"I don't *feel* like doing this all goddamn night, Betty Jean, I really don't, but —" He stood his ground, shaking his head at her, conviction in his eyes. He took a deep breath, holding her look. "I'm *prepared* to do this all night, BJ. Just don't make me have to, all right?"

She could see in his face that he meant the words, but still she shrugged. What the fuck did that mean? *Don't make me have to.* What-the-fuck-ever, she thought to herself, before saying, "I'm *not* doing this all goddamned night, whether you're prepared to or not. In fact, I'm not doing this another second. Now move, so I can go into the other room."

He didn't budge.

"Give me the card, Betty Jean."

"Leave me alone about it, Ezekiel," she said, in the same tone he'd used.

"Betty Jean."

"Ezekiel." She folded her arms across her chest. "Now that we know one another's names, can we move on?"

He stood a moment longer, then sighed. "Shit." In one swift motion he grabbed the belt loops on both sides of her jeans, jerked her towards him and turned her around, reaching for the pocket that held the card.

In the brief second that he had Betty Jean's back pressed to his front, she drew back her right foot and her K*Swiss tennis shoe connected neatly with his knee cap. He went down, but didn't relinquish his hold on her clothing. When he toppled to the thick carpet, he pulled her down with him. Ezekiel tried to turn her as they fell, causing Betty Jean to land half on the carpeted floor and half across him. His hands grabbed and pulled at the pocket she tried to protect.

"Stop it, goddamnit!" she screamed. He was deaf to her struggles and threats, intent on his objective. "Let me go!" She slammed her elbow into his stomach, but he twisted away from the blow and she landed a glancing strike only. She pulled, trying to rise and he tugged, trying to prevent it. Fabric ripped and the left belt loop hung drunkenly from her jeans.

With a final jab and a surge of angry strength, Betty Jean regained her feet. Her hair was disheveled and she brushed a clump of it away from her eyes. "What the fuck is wrong with you?" she demanded, glaring at Ezekiel as he began to rise. "Don't ever put your fucking hands on me like that again, Ezekiel," she said as she walked into the bedroom.

"What's up on that card? What's so important that you'd rather fight me than let me see it?" He was leaning in the doorway of the room when she turned to face him, trying to keep his weight off of the injured leg. His knee was throbbing, but he ignored it.

"It's not about fighting you. It's just none of your damn business. You have all types of shit you hide from me on a daily basis and I'm straight with that. You want to be a sneaky little fucker? Fine. Be one. But then don't go losing your damn mind over a funky ass card someone gives me. You're not supposed to sweat this kind of shit anyway. You the player, remember? Play on then and get out of mine." She snatched the band from her hair, letting whatever hadn't already come loose in their struggle fall about her shoulders.

"So, another man did leave you that card?" He heard only what he wanted to hear. Her remarks of him being a player were left untouched. They commonly ignored that particular elephant that lived in their living room and she was really tripping trying to drag that shit into it right now. They were way out here in California. Who was he going to *play on* with?

"Why is it, *so another man did*, just because I mentioned the shit you do? Who are you hiding from me, Ezekiel? How many people are in the bed with us at night? Who's on your mind?"

"Today isn't about me, BJ."

She raised her eyebrows at his comment. "Isn't it? Everything has been about you for years now. I'm just the fucking sidekick in your little adventures and melodramas. I only exist because of you. Solely for your benefit, didn't you know? Your fucking Tonto."

Though her words dripped sarcasm, his reply was straight forward enough. "You say it like it's a bad thing. What's wrong with living for me? It never seemed to bother you before. Who made it seem so terrible? Ole boy with the card?"

"You did!" She shot back, angry. "You did, goddamnit! Do I mind living for you? No. Do I mind being a fool for you? Yes. Do I mind blindly turning my head while someone else fucks my man? Yes. Do I feel like another second loving you will be too long? That it would kill me? Yes, goddamnit, yes! And no one made me think like that but you, Ezekiel. If you have to know, yes, the card is from a man. He's an option. Something opposed to you and your continuous bullshit."

"So, what? You think letting someone else love you, touch you, would make what you feel for me go away?" He could not believe they were having this conversation. His BJ, taking numbers from strangers, talking about her fucking options.

"Actually, Ezekiel, I know for a fact that letting another man love me, touch me, make love to me, will not make what I feel for you go away," she said the words softly, a simple statement of fact and there was a hidden sadness in her eyes.

His eyes raked her from head to toe and back again. Slowly he began to shake his head in denial. "What did you do, Betty Jean?"

"Like you always tell me, *nothing.* I didn't do anything that should matter to us, right? That's the kind of couple we are. Nothing you do affects us. We just keep rolling merrily along. Hell, what could *I* have possibly done that would cause a ripple in the beautiful calm that is us?"

"What did you do, Betty Jean?"

She turned from him and he grabbed her shoulders, spinning her back around to face him. "Betty Jean." She jerked loose from his touch and in a flash he had her pinned against the wall. His full length pressed against her body. He stood for a moment with his forehead resting against the wall behind her.

"Tell me what you did, Betty Jean. Tell me you gave yourself to another man, that you let some nigga fuck you. What you let him do to you, Betty Jean? What you do to him?" His voice was calm, conversational.

Hers was even calmer. "Tell me why you missed our flight. What was so important that you left me hanging without a word?" Tears danced in her eyes, but she refused to let them fall. When she'd done what she did last night, she hadn't thought it through to the end. To what would happen if or when Ezekiel found out. She was hurt and angry that their argument was even taking place, but she refused to bend. Even if what she'd done was wrong, who was he to demand and dictate as often as he brought a wet dick to her bed?

His hand came up between them, wrapping around her neck like a snake. "You bitch," he said the words so softly, she barely heard them above the blood surging in her ears. "You fucked someone else, a stranger, because I missed a plane?" He stared at her incredulously.

Betty Jean swallowed and could feel his hand against her throat, restricting the movement. Still she whispered, "No. I fucked someone else because I needed to be held and touched and wanted. And you were too busy to get on the goddamned plane!"

His hand dropped from her throat and he backed away, staring at her as though for the first time. He couldn't believe it. His Betty Jean out fucking around on him and he'd been feeling like shit about Carla. Even last night, he hadn't touched her. It had been Betty Jean he wanted and she'd been out fucking someone else. He felt like a fool. Betrayed and stupid. While he'd been going through a crisis, needing her, hurting over the loss of his child, she'd been out acting like a harlot. He stepped away from her, but still continued to stare in muted disbelief. Finally, he turned, walked into the outer room, picked up his bag from where he'd dropped it that morning and left the suite.

Eleven

"*The battle is not yours, it's the Lord's. It's the Lord's.*" Sheila sung one of her favorite gospel tunes as she walked through the office preparing for her day. She was resplendent in a Bill Blass pants suit of deep purple linen. Her feet were covered in the softest leather and the shoes matched her outfit perfectly. As did her nails, which were deep purple with a lavender diamond studded diagonal line on both ring fingers.

She'd spent the entire weekend curled around, under and over Spencer and she was floating on sunshine. *Walking is an exercise in itself*, she thought, smiling to herself, *but floating is just fine.*

"Umph, I'm going to miss that man," she said out loud as she let herself into Betty Jean's office to place Friday's mail on her desk. It was only 7:30 in the morning on Monday and Betty Jean wasn't due back at work until the next morning, but Sheila didn't like sitting with her back to the dark office. She always had the feeling someone was lurking in the darkness waiting for her. She blamed it on an overactive imagination and two older brothers with too much time on their hands as children, but she stuck to the ritual just the same. She would go in, turn the lights on and open up the blinds.

Stepping into the office, she flicked on the overhead lights and screamed, dropping the mail to the carpet. A hand to her racing heart, she leaned against the door for support. "Betty Jean Carlson! What in the hell are you doing here? And sitting in the dark, scaring years off my life?"

"You scared me!" Betty Jean accused. "Walking in here screaming like that! And at seven-thirty in the morning!" she teased, imitating her assistant's surprise.

Sheila, having recovered, marched across the office, one hand on her hip and the other shaking a finger at her boss. "Oh, no you don't. No, ma'am, you aren't going to change the subject that easily. Yes, I know you prefer to work in the dark in the mornings and I come in early when you aren't here. So, we can see something is amiss. One of us isn't supposed to be here. One of us should be in California, lying in bed with her man and the other should be here at work. Or one of us should be at my apartment still lying in bed with Spencer. How did we get it confused?"

She stood staring at Betty Jean. Her finger, having stopped wagging, went limp as she folded her arms across her chest, intent on waiting. When Betty Jean remained silent, Sheila lifted one finely arched brow and pressed, "Betty Jean, why are you here?"

"I came back yesterday."

"Ahhh, the simply stated," she said, nodding her head in appreciation of the art. "Not going to work, BJ. Come on, it's getting late. Everyone will be here soon. You aren't supposed to be here until tomorrow and I didn't get a juicy detail-packed call last night about the wonders of California. And," she dragged out the word, taking a deep breath finally, "you said *I came back yesterday*. Not good. How did *I* come back when *we* left?"

Betty Jean turned away from the computer screen, giving up all pretense of work. She swung her chair around to face the window. "We didn't leave Thursday, I left Thursday. Ezekiel showed up the next morning. He got mad at me. We had a fight and he left that same evening. I stayed the weekend then came to work this morning." She hunched her shoulders, continuing to look out the window.

"Whoa," Sheila exhaled loudly, her eyebrows rising. "What did you guys fight about that would make him that angry? He just got on a flight and left California?"

"I don't know." Betty Jean's shoulders drooped. Both women were silent for a moment, each contemplating the bullshit of Betty Jean's *I don't know.* Sheila knew damn well Betty Jean knew exactly why Ezekiel left the West Coast, but if she didn't want to talk about it, it was cool.

Betty Jean was like that. When Sheila was pissed off, she'd rant and rave, spilling her guts to her girlfriends, but not Betty Jean. Betty Jean's business was her business and she never shared. She played her cards close to the vest. No one was going to see them until she laid them on the table. Problem was, Sheila thought looking at Betty Jean's profile, she never laid them down. She just kept them clutched in her own two hands.

Betty Jean was thinking similar thoughts. When she returned home last night, she'd walked into an empty house and she would have dearly loved to have called someone and wept. Just simply wept, she was so hurt. What had she done? Took a bold new step or stepped on six years worth of love? Yes, last night she would have loved to unburden herself to a friend, but she couldn't do it. Even now, all she wanted was to turn and spill her heart to Sheila, but her lips pressed together, working to hold her secrets in, instead of releasing them.

She shook her head slowly. She couldn't tell. She couldn't let the world know how stupid she'd been. How stupid she still was. How weak. No. She was not going to be the pathetic fool whose back everyone whispered behind and felt sorry for.

No one would ever know how Ezekiel had hurt her and he'd hurt her bad. Betty Jean felt the tears roll down her face and brushed them aside with her fingers. *No use in crying*, she told herself, but that failed to stop the moisture from gathering in her eyes and spilling over again. She put her face in her hands and bent over. A small sob escaped her throat.

Sheila rushed to close the office door and lock it. She hurried back to Betty Jean. Dropping to one knee, she pulled Betty Jean's hands from her face. "No, ma'am, you are not going to sit there and cry like that, like no one cares about you. Look, honey, we may not be super close and that's your choice not mine, but girl, you can talk to me. Nothing you tell me will cross my lips again."

Betty Jean wrapped her arms around herself, squeezed her eyes shut and continued to cry. Sheila rubbed her back in soothing circles. "If you don't want to talk to me, call your mother or your preacher." Sheila was surprised by her own suggestions. The pastor of her church was a formidable looking man that she couldn't see going to for anything. He was too powerful, too intimidating. And tell mama something deep and personal? The thought of confessing her sins and troubles to Pastor Theodore Givens or Mrs. Roslyn Cooper made her shrink inwardly. She loved Roslyn and they were close, but she still couldn't see giving her the key to her business.

At Sheila's suggestion, Betty Jean thought of her mother and cried harder. Sheila had been her assistant for over a year now and Betty Jean had never told her both her parents were deceased. The only person who knew so intimate a thing about her life was the same person who had her in tears now. Ezekiel.

Unaware, Sheila kept rubbing Betty Jean's back and talking. "Write it down on paper if you have to," she suggested, "but any way it's done, it needs to be done. You can't lock everything away like it doesn't hurt you because girl, pain does not like to be ignored. It will make itself known. Find a way to release it. Tears only work for so long."

Sheila could see a shadow moving through the frosted panel on either side of Betty Jean's office door and excused herself to ward off the intruder. When she returned, Betty Jean had collected herself enough to at least stop crying and was once again facing her computer screen.

"I slept with someone else." Her voice was soft, placid. Sheila stopped mid stride. Betty Jean let her gaze travel from the computer screen to rest on Sheila. She nodded her head in affirmation of what she'd just said. "That's why we fought. That's why he left. I slept with another man."

Sheila sat down in one of the chairs facing the big desk. After careful thought, she asked, "Do you want to tell me about it?"

Betty Jean's smile wobbled. "No. I don't want to tell anybody about this. I want to bury my humiliation where no one will ever see it." She shook her head in wonder. "You wouldn't believe what I've put up with, Sheila. The bullshit I allowed him to get away with, over and over again. How I shared him." Without much flare Betty Jean told Sheila about her life with Ezekiel. She withheld nothing. She was tired of keeping shit in and hiding it.

Throughout the telling, Sheila remained silent. Her job was to listen; to be a sounding board. There was plenty that she wanted to say. Being a single female herself, she loved her bullshit-free existence and there was no way in hell she'd put up with such shit. Fine as he was, Zeke would have found himself kissing the curb a long time ago.

Betty Jean was right, too. Sheila *couldn't* believe she was letting him wreck her up. He was not worth all the drama and she wasn't able to stop herself from saying so. She may not offer advice, but she could still state the obvious. Ezekiel had lost all favor with her. The jackass.

Betty Jean looked down at her hands, whispering, "I love him, Sheila."

Sheila sat quietly looking at her friend. Betty Jean was a good person who always tried to do right by people. It was sad that she carried around such weight, but Sheila knew from long experiences with her sisters and other girlfriends, that no amount of anything was going to make Betty Jean walk away until she'd had enough. It would be a waste of breath and energy to suggest that, because there would always be some excuse for holding on. Betty Jean had already stated hers. She loved Ezekiel Johnson. Sheila guessed that was reason enough as far as Betty Jean was concerned. As long as she was in love, she would put up with his shit.

Sheila doubted if it would be enough for her, but then she was single and planned to stay that way. She didn't know one happy couple, not a single one. Hell, Betty Jean and her man were her Cinderella story. Whenever she thought about a happy couple the two of them would come to mind, but now that was shot to hell.

The phone rang in the outer office and Sheila stood to answer it. Just before she reached the door, she stopped. Turning, she asked, "Betty Jean, does this satisfy you? This little piece of happiness that he's giving you, or *was* giving you. Is it enough? This little piece?"

Betty Jean looked at her, considering the question. "It used to be." Sheila opened the door, passing through it when Betty Jean added, "That's a lie. I used to pretend that it was enough, but sharing Ezekiel has never been what I wanted. I was never happy with that part of him."

Sheila looked at her, nodding her head in understanding, then pulled the door closed behind her.

**

It was after two in the afternoon when Sheila knocked at the door to Betty Jean's office. Her hands were filled, so she tapped at the door with the square toe of her purple boot. "Help, please!" she called out.

"What's this?" Betty Jean laughed as she stepped aside, allowing Sheila to enter the office.

Sheila sat on the couch pulling items from various bags. "Chinese, girl. We have to eat! That Moo Goo Mess you like." She held up a container. "Some fried rice with everything thrown in it, but that nasty pork." She made a face at the thought of eating swine. "Beef broccoli and curry chicken for me. *And*," she dragged the word out as she reached into another bag, "–lock that door, we don't want anybody walking in–one really cold Skyy Blue." She held the blue bottle low as she poured the liquid into two Styrofoam cups.

Betty Jean laughed as she seated herself across from Sheila and kicked off her shoes. "I can't believe you bought us a beer to share."

Sheila shrugged, not the least bit contrite. "I felt something extra was in order, today."

"Well, the next time you think we need something extra in our day, bring two." Betty Jean sipped from her cup. She wasn't an advocate for drinking on the job, but like Sheila, she too felt something extra was in order for the day. She grabbed one of the cartons spread out on the coffee table and a set of chopsticks. She slung her legs over the arm of her chair and dug into the food. She hadn't eaten all day and it smelled wonderful. She hadn't realized she had such an appetite. Unloading herself on Sheila felt therapeutic. She thought that once she told what was going on in her life, she'd feel ashamed and wouldn't be able to look at her confessor, but that wasn't the case at all.

Sheila made her feel like she was speaking to someone who may not understand first hand what she was going through, but cared enough to listen, and Betty Jean didn't think her story would turn up on the six o' clock news after having been spread all across the office. She was more at ease and felt lighter than she had in a long time.

Sheila looked at her smiling, her eyes twinkling with their usual mischief. "You feeling better, honey?"

Betty Jean nodded, her mouth filled with Moo Goo. Sheila's smile grew and she sat back with the carton of fried rice. "Good. Now stop playing and tell me about the fine ass brother you met in California!"

**

"You want to go do something tonight?"

Carla shrugged her shoulders, frowning. She was putting twists in the front of her hair in an intricate design and the hair kept slipping through her fingers.

"We can go see a movie or go to Frankie's." He didn't really feel like Frankie's, but with darts, pool tables and slot machines, there'd be something interesting to do. Carla had been fooling around with her hair ever since he got in from work and it was beginning to irritate the shit out of him. He was used to Betty Jean's full attention and even Carla's or at least the attention she used to give him. Now her attitude towards him bordered between nonchalant and tolerant and he was getting sick of it. "You want me to leave, Carla? Just say so, you don't usually bite your tongue."

Carla's eyes met Zeke's in the mirror above the sink. "Are you trying to pick a fight with me? If so, I don't feel like it, so squash the noise." She put a rubber band around the end of the twist she'd just completed and turned to face him, shrugging her shoulders in question.

"What do you expect me to do, Zeke? How happy can I be that you're here? You're only here sulking over some shit that happened between you and your girl. Had the two of you not gotten into it, you wouldn't be here, would you? No, you wouldn't. I'm not crazy, Zeke, I just play like it on television," she said, paraphrasing the old commercial. "You aren't here to stay. You're just crashing here until one of you cools off enough to call the other one."

"I'm here right now, though, Carla. You can at least act like you care."

"I'm here right now, too, so why are you tripping? Why don't you handle whatever it is you're trying to deal with and quit taking your funky ass moods out on me, all right? I can't keep playing cheerleader for you, Zeke and reassuring your madness every few hours until I'm insane, too."

He didn't know if he liked the *new Carla*, as he'd been referring to her over the past six days. The old Carla was always talking shit, but with an undercurrent of playfulness and sexuality. He'd never taken anything sassy she said seriously. It was just her style, but there was nothing humorous in the new Carla, especially not in the way she spoke to him. The new Carla always sounded like she meant whatever she was saying and didn't give a damn about how he took it.

Back in the day, she would have had her hair done long before he showed up. She would have been looking good, smelling good and totally focused on him, but he'd been at her place since Saturday and received none of that. Yeah, she still looked good and put her shit down and all that, but he didn't feel as though she did it just for him anymore.

He missed Betty Jean like hell and the new Carla wasn't helping matters any. In the near week since he'd last seen Betty Jean, he'd thought about what she'd done a lot. A part of him still couldn't believe it. It was too unreal. But the part of him that did believe, felt guilty. He knew that had he been where he was supposed to be, Betty Jean's indiscretion would never have taken place. No other man would have known the silky feel of his BJ.

Yes, Ezekiel thought, he was as much to blame as she was, but the other guy...his blame was the largest. He'd taken advantage of Betty Jean when she was feeling low. Ezekiel knew that could be the only way his Betty Jean would have betrayed him. She was upset because he missed the flight, had probably been out somewhere drinking and then some dime store Casanova had come along and taken advantage of her.

It was sad really, that some men were like that. Willing to prey on innocent women when they were at their most vulnerable. Even sadder still, that his own sweetheart had fallen victim. His pride didn't sting as hotly as it did when he stormed out of California, but he still wasn't sure if he could forgive her. He needed more time to think. Which the new Carla wasn't making easy. How was he supposed to figure out what he wanted when she wasn't treating him the way she used to, the right way?

"Let's get something to eat, then go to Frankie's and shoot pool," he said finally, then turned from the door without waiting on her response.

Twelve

It's never a good thing when I come in and you're facing that window. I mean, it's a great view from up here, but it's still never a good sign when I come in and you're facing towards it, trying to soak up the peace." Sheila came into the office placing two files on the coffee table. She was dressed in a long, lavender, mermaid-pleated skirt styled from the nineteen forties with matching lavender pumps and a simple white blouse. She looked very ladylike and very professional. Her hair was swept into a sophisticated French twist. She was feeling very feminine in her outfit and it showed in her walk, to which any male in the building could attest.

Sheila put her hands on her hips. Staring at the back of Betty Jean's head, she scowled. Before she could open her mouth to speak again, Betty Jean turned slowly in her chair asking, "Could you be ready to leave in less than two weeks time?" Her eyes met Sheila's, who sank gracefully into one of the chairs she'd been standing beside and held.

"Come again?" she asked.

"Charles called this morning," Betty Jean explained, referring to the only partner she'd had any communication with, Charles Hurstwode. They'd spoken enough since his original job offer that they'd moved past the formality of surnames. "The board agreed to my terms. They want us to get a fresh start at the beginning of next month, but they have a few important meetings that they'd like me to sit in on during the last week of this month. That gives us just under two weeks. We'd need to be out of here by the end of next week. What do you think, super assistant?" Betty Jean referred to the moniker she'd given Sheila long ago, when she'd discovered Sheila's talent for making the impossible look like a walk in the park. Another reason she found her irreplaceable. "Can it be done?"

"They agreed to your demands?"

"I wasn't holding anyone hostage, Sheila. You make it sound like I called to tell them where the ransom should be left." It was close, but she saw no reason to bring that up. She'd only told Sheila half of the story the first time. It was true that Hurstwode and Donovan made her a job offer, but by the time Hurstwode contacted Betty Jean for the first time the board had already made up its mind to hire her. The delay was caused by Betty Jean's desire to bring Sheila along and at such a substantial salary increase. Betty Jean told them she'd take the position but only under her terms, which included the doubling of Sheila's salary.

Not ransom, Betty Jean thought, just good business.

Sheila sat in silence for a moment, mentally going over the clients they had and what work they were in the middle of processing, deciding whom she should dump it all on. She flipped through the calendar in her mind, seeing Betty Jean's schedule clearly. It would take at least two associates to handle Betty Jean's work load, but it could be done. A slow smile spread across her face. "Girlfriend, for double my current salary, I could have us living in another country under assumed names in less than twenty-four hours. Being ready to wave goodbye to this place by next Friday will be a cinch" Betty Jean saw a flash of dark purple when Sheila twisted her fingers in a snap.

"The more I think on it, the more I like the idea of leaving most of my things behind and just starting over from scratch. It would be cheaper than moving my furniture and I know I'm going to want new shit anyway. Something that reflects my new lifestyle. Something sunny and California-ish."

"That may be a good idea, leaving everything behind. Shoot, you'd need a fleet of trucks to ship your boxes of clothes alone. Then another fleet for your shoes and accessories!" Betty Jean laughed, delighting in the moment. She knew Sheila would forsake her move to California long before she gave up her clothes and shoes.

Sheila looked comically shocked, before laughing, too. "They were never in danger of being left behind. *Never,*" she stretched out the word, regaining her look of shocked dismay. "I can't even believe you would suggest such a thing! Even joking. *Leave my clothes behind,*" she repeated incredulously. She looked at Betty Jean skeptically, as though having never noticed the other woman's insanity. "Would a mother leave her children? I was only referring to my furniture. It would just be plain cheaper to leave it. There's no point in going through the expense of moving it; especially when I know I'm going to shop like a mad woman once we hit the West Coast! Girl!" She stomped her feet soundlessly and opened her mouth in a silent scream, shaking her head from side to side in a mute display of excitement. Then finally, nearly shouting, she said, "We're going to the wild, wild west!"

**

Carla was in the middle of dressing for work when someone knocked at the front door. Cursing, she pushed her arms through the sleeves in her shirt. When her head popped through the opening she made her way to the front of the apartment. Looking through the peephole, she could only see the fist as it contacted with the door again, pounding just above the circular opening she had her eye pressed against. She jerked away from the noise. "Who is it?" she demanded, suspicious of the unexpected guest.

"Me. Open the door."

Recognizing the voice, she stepped behind the door as she pulled it open. All she had on was her work shirt that stopped just at the curve of her behind and she wasn't trying to flash the neighborhood.

"What's up?" she asked, locking the door back. "Why didn't you use your key? I don't have time to be running to the door." She turned as if to go back in to the other room, when his voice stopped her.

"Use my key? Stop tripping. How am I supposed to just walk up in here when you got someone posted up with you?"

Carla rolled her eyes at the topic of discussion and hurried from the room. "I don't have time this morning for a well deep conversation, Thom, so if you have to say something, say it, but say it fast."

Thomas followed Carla to her bedroom. Stopping at the entrance he tried hard to keep his eyes from traveling. He didn't want them to fall upon evidence of the other man, so he kept his gaze on Carla. "You won't let me come over and take you to work. I understand that. You're trying to do your independent thing. Your I-don't-need-my-baby's-daddy thing and that's cool, but what's ole boy's excuse? If he's lying in here with you, why isn't he keeping you off the bus?" He used *if* hoping that he'd guessed wrong. Wanting her to correct him.

He'd never met the cat Carla was slinking around with, but he'd seen his car enough to recognize it. That car had been parked in front of Carla's all night, every night, for the last week, which wasn't usual. Thomas had seen the car there plenty of times before, but dude always went home. Not recently. Thomas made the assumption that something had changed between the two of them, but he'd waited to talk to Carla, because he wanted to be wrong. But standing in the apartment, he could feel the truth. Carla *was* living with someone else.

Carla sighed, looking down at the pants she'd just pulled on, and took them off. They needed ironing badly. She couldn't even pretend like she could still see a crease in them. "He goes to work before I do. Way before I do, so giving me a ride to work isn't an option. Before you say it," she cut him off, knowing his next line of attack, "no, I can't drop him off because he's ready to go by five and needs his car. I can't leave work to go get him."

She could have told him that Ezekiel usually picked her up from work, since he was off by then and still didn't have a key to her apartment. She hadn't had time to get a key made for him yet, and wasn't all that certain she wanted to find the time. Giving Zeke a key to her place would mean taking Thomas's key away. And she wanted to do that less than she wanted to give a key to Ezekiel.

Thom had always had a key to her place. What if he needed to get something for Ebony and she wasn't home? What if he needed to drop something off? Carla frowned at the direction her thoughts had gone and made a mental effort to push them aside. She didn't like thinking about Thom sometimes. It made her head hurt. She touched a finger to the still too cool iron, then turned to go into the bathroom. She could finish her hair while the iron heated.

"Carla, come here," Thomas called from the bedroom doorway, where he'd stopped earlier. He didn't want to go into a room she was currently sharing with someone else.

"I have to get ready, Thom. I'm already pressed for time," her voice floated to him from the bathroom.

Thomas set his jaw, gritting his teeth. He walked across the bedroom, reached into the bathroom and pulled Carla out. As they passed her armoire, he took the brush from her unresisting hand and placed it there. Thomas threaded his fingers through hers as he led her into the living room, seating her on the couch.

He sat on the edge of the coffee table facing her. Their joined hands were suspended in the space between them. Thomas had his head bowed, heavy with thought. Carla couldn't tell whether he stared at their hands, his shoes, the carpet or if he saw anything at all. He just sat transfixed and she was loathe to break the silence. She knew Thomas well enough to know he had something serious to say. He was simply trying to work out how to get it said. As time was an issue that morning, she couldn't wait him out. She squeezed his fingers slightly in encouragement and in an effort to move things along. Care and concern aside, she didn't have time for this shit.

Thomas said, "I'm giving you a ride to work, so chill out little mama," and Carla's eyes widened in guilt. Had she spoken that last shit aloud? Damn, she needed to stop smoking, she berated herself. She couldn't think straight. Already this morning, she'd blown half a strawberry philly.

Ezekiel was working her nerves, though. He'd gotten up that morning bitching about breakfast. Breakfast! At seven o'clock in the morning! Everyday he was getting crazier. Her baby girl had gone from her daddy's house to her granny's, so fixing breakfast hadn't been foremost in Carla's mind. Besides, Ebony had adapted to Carla's schedule and neither one of them was up at seven in the morning. So, even if her daughter had been home, Carla would never have thought to cook that early.

It didn't help that Carla didn't particularly care for breakfast and with the hours that she worked, she simply didn't have to be up that damned early. Why in the hell would she give a rat's ass about breakfast? But apparently Ezekiel thought she should, because he kept trying to encourage her to make it for him and kept bitching when she didn't.

This morning she rolled her breakfast as soon as he left the house and lit it on one end. She usually held her fire until later in the day, but again, Ezekiel was working her nerves to no end. So, not only did he have her awake too damned early in the morning, he had her smoking too damned early, too. Had her thinking about giving up an old friend. She pouted, not liking the idea of quitting smoking. Mary Jane was her girl. One of her oldest friends. True, she didn't like the way her habit was increasing, but damn, Zeke was making her crazy and smoking was the only thing keeping her hands from circling around his throat. Her hand itched for the remaining half of her sweet.

"What's up on you and ole boy?" Thomas asked, breaking into her thoughts.

"What's up, Thomas?" Carla countered with a question of her own, avoiding his. Hell, she didn't know what was up with anything or anybody. She hadn't thought Ezekiel would last as long as he had. When he'd shown up on her doorstep with his bags, she'd almost laughed in his face, it was so ridiculous. All of a sudden he wanted to leave Betty Country Jean and get something serious started with her. No explanations, either, just some bullshit about rethinking his commitments. What-the-fuck-ever.

Ezekiel was cool and all, but after all the shit she put up with from him over the last year, she didn't know if she wanted to step back into his game. Okay, he was rethinking his commitments, but all she wanted to know was why he hadn't thought about them before she killed her child? She knew it was an unfair thought, since he hadn't even known that she was pregnant until it was too late, but she couldn't seem to help how she felt. Whenever she thought about what happened, she got angry at Ezekiel. Had he been handling his business right in the first place, he —

Her thoughts of Ezekiel were again interrupted by Thomas. "Look, Carla, I'm not trying to get into your business or anything like that. I'm just trying to find out what's going on." Thomas shook his head. Nothing was coming out the way he wanted. He wanted to know why Carla was letting some motherfucker post up at her house and just what that shit meant. He wanted to talk about his little girl. He hadn't ever thought about his Ebony doll being raised by some other cat. He was still in the picture and always would be when it came to his little sweetheart, but if Carla was going to be living with someone else, then that man was going to be in Ebony's life, too. He didn't like that shit at all. He cut for that idea even less than he did for sharing Carla's attentions. Damn, he couldn't believe that they'd gotten to the point where – fuck, he trailed off. He couldn't think clearly. Thomas dropped Carla's hand and stood, pacing the living room.

"What's wrong, Thomas?"

He stopped mid-circle, turning to face her. "You living here with someone else for starters, Carla. That shit's wrong, wrong, wrong. Second, my baby girl will be back in a couple of days and she's coming home to her mama and some tack-head I ain't never even met." He counted off each offense, holding up a finger as he listed each. "Third, I'm losing my girls all over again and last, I don't know how to not care about you, C. I've kept you right here." With a fist he tapped his chest, just above his heart.

"Damn, girl, I can't believe I'm about to lose you. I don't have anybody to blame, except myself, so I can't even get mad about it. I can only be hurt. Really, really hurt and I think I might die." His words came out in a rush and he crossed the room, seating himself on the couch with his head in his hands when he stopped speaking. His voice was calm when he spoke again. His words were slowed by resignation to a situation he was powerless to change. "Seriously, Carla, sometimes, I feel like I can't breathe from wanting you so much. I just want you to love me again."

Carla stared at him beside her on the couch. She opened her mouth to speak more than once, but kept closing it. She was completely floored by Thomas's declarations and wasn't really certain of how to respond.

He'd said he was losing both his girls. So he hadn't realized she'd been gone from him all this time? Carla asked the question softly. She wasn't trying to be sarcastic or hurtful, she was just surprised and needed to understand what the hell was going on. The marijuana in her system wasn't making comprehension an easy task. She didn't feel like sobering up, so he was going to have to break it down for her in its simplest form if he wanted her to get it.

Thomas's look was pure exasperation. "You need to stop smoking that shit, Carla, for real. It's messing your head up. You're not half as smart high as you are when you're not smoking. Yeah, I knew you were gone, retarded girl. I just never felt that you were lost from me, you know? We broke up or whatever," he raised his shoulders against the words he'd never accepted, "but you and Ebony were still mine." When he finally looked up, his eyes searched Carla's for understanding before plunging in again.

"I love you, Carla. I did some stupid shit that made you leave me, but I hadn't lost you. I never stopped loving you. Never. Nobody's ever meant to me what you do. I doubt if anyone ever will." He ducked his head again not wanting to see her face when he said his next words. *What if he saw relief in her eyes?* "I'll let go. I mean, you do your own thing now, but old Thom is still yours. I'm just sitting here waiting for you. Waiting for you to love me again," he repeated the words he'd spoken a moment before, then paused, considering telling her everything. About how he hadn't been with anyone since her and hadn't wanted anybody else.

He wanted to tell her his plans for the future. What he'd decided for himself. But he didn't. He didn't want to influence whatever she said. "I'll kill all that noise," he said hesitating for a moment. *Could he really*? He thought. *Let go of all he felt for Carla?* Yeah, he could do it, if it would make her happy.

He took a deep breath and said again more firmly, "I'll kill all of it, Carla. Everything I feel for you will be a thing of the past if that's what you want. I care about you. I'll do whatever I have to, wait as long as it takes, in order to get my family back, but I don't want to spend forever waiting on something I'll never have. So, if you're serious about this cat and you won't be coming back to me, tell me now, so I can finally open up my hands."

And let me go, Carla concluded his thought.

Did she really want that? True, she'd left Thomas, but they were still together in many ways. She could blame the time they spent together on Ebony, but she wouldn't be telling the truth. They'd spent time together with Ebony at the ice skating rink, Chuck E. Cheese, the movies. All places she could have easily gone with one parent, but they usually went together. As a family. Thomas was always there when she needed something, though in her stubbornness she tried to not need anything. She just took his presence for granted and went about her way.

She'd never actually thought of having to give that luxury up. She didn't know what Thom's romantic life was like and had no desire to find out, but he'd never even hinted at there being other women. Of course, she wasn't naive enough to believe she'd been the last person he'd had sex with. She knew Thom and doubted he'd been sitting around all this time, playing with his dick, waiting on her. Not Thomas. They used to be hot and heavy all the time. Thomas was always touching her or pulling her towards him for a kiss or a rub. No doubt he was the same with others.

She figured he had other women, but like her, hadn't found anyone to fill that spot, yet. That special place. Carla knew he still cared for her. It was obvious. But she hadn't known he still felt the exact same way about her as he always had. That even after she closed herself off to him, he was still loving her. Still waiting on her.

She never let herself examine what she felt for him. She'd wrapped herself in her hurt and anger and stayed there, never letting enough light in to see how her feelings for him fared. *Did she want Thomas to let go of her? Did she want the normal That's-just-my-baby's-daddy relationship? Drop off the kid and leave like they hate each other*? Hell, Carla thought, she knew she didn't want that.

Thomas was her — He was her — Shit. She didn't know what Thomas was to her and didn't really want to scratch the surface deep enough to find out. *Was she still in love with him?* She didn't know. Thomas hurt her and she had swaddled herself up pretty tight. All she knew was that he was pissing her off. Scaring the shit out of her with all this talk of opening his hands and letting go of her.

Ten minutes passed and they still sat. Neither of them dared to break the silence, too afraid of what the other had to say.

Finally, it was Thomas who spoke first. Rising from the couch he said, "Go ahead and get dressed for work, little mama. I'll be out here waiting."

Carla rose from the couch and stood facing him. She wanted to say something, but wasn't sure what would be the right thing. *How long will you wait for me? Please don't let me go. Stop scaring me.* She shook her head against the various possibilities that came to mind and left Thomas standing in the middle of the living room staring at a picture of them taken at the school prom years ago. She was smiling up at him with love written all over her face.

**

"Are you going to be home this evening about six o'clock?" He'd asked the question without preamble, as soon as she answered the phone.

It took Betty Jean a moment to identify the voice as Ezekiel's. "I'm doing fine, thank you for asking."

"I didn't call you to start an argument. I only wanted to know if you'll be at the house, so I can come by."

"I wasn't trying to start an argument with you either. Merely drawing attention to the apparent fact that I no longer merit common courtesy. I feel like one of the poor souls in Paradise Lost, kicked from the kingdom. How far the mighty have fallen."

There was a pause on the other end and then softly he said, "If I ask how you're doing, I might care to know the answer. So I didn't ask."

"So, what are you coming to the house for? To get the rest of your things? So, we can talk? What?" She waited for the answer, holding her breath.

"I don't know. I know I need some more clothes, but I don't know if I need to get everything just yet."

She let the breath she was holding out with more than a little bit of irritation. "Well, you do whatever you need to do, Ezekiel. You have a key to the house, so you can come and go at will. Just like you've always done. You never waited for my permission before, you don't need it now!" She hung up the phone, sick of his bullshit.

He didn't know if he needed to get everything just yet, she mimicked his voice, repeating his words. She guessed she was supposed to sit around crying and upset, trying to figure out a way to get back into his good graces.

Betty Jean reached into the cupboard, wrapping the last wine glass in bubble wrap and placing it into the box on the counter. She'd been wrapping, taping, boxing, folding and basically working her butt off since she got *off* work Friday. Her goal was to have the house near to completion by Sunday night. She wouldn't have time during the week to get much done. She and Sheila had been working twelve hour days since Hurstwode and Donovan called. Thursday would be their last day in the office, but with the hours they'd put in last week their work load would be completed by Tuesday. She already arranged for the moving truck. It would be at her house early Friday morning and at Sheila's by late afternoon.

She had an action-packed week planned and wouldn't have time to still be wrapping plates. She wouldn't have time for any of Ezekiel's bullshit, either. She would make a point of being at the house at six. She needed to know what to tell the movers. *Were they loading his belongings as well as hers? Or had he changed his mind about going to California? Were they over or did he just need some time to think? As many times as she'd forgiven him, was he really going to withhold his forgiveness from her?* She didn't know, but she was getting damned tired of worrying about it.

Thirteen

So, are you going to be quiet all night?" Ezekiel glanced over to Carla, then back to the road. He'd picked her up from work and other than the hello she'd given when she first got in the car, she hadn't spoken.

"I'm sorry, Zeke. I have a lot going on inside my head."

"Yeah? What's wrong, pretty lady?" His voice was laced with genuine concern. He hadn't thought about it before, but whatever was on her mind could be her reason for treating him so indifferently. Maybe if he could help her solve her problems, she'd be able to refocus on him. With new resolve he pressed, "Talk to me, Carla. If we're going to make our relationship work we need to be able to talk to one another." He put his arm around Carla's shoulders in a quick gesture of reassurance. "I want to know when something's wrong with my girl."

Carla turned her head, looking out the passenger window. "Am I your girl, Ezekiel? That's one of the biggest issues on my mind lately. What are we doing? What are *you* doing? Do you even know? Are you going back to Betty Jean?" She raised her shoulders against the weight of her questions, shaking her head wearily. "I'm just getting too old for all of this, you know? What happens when I'm twenty-five? Or thirty? Thirty-five?" She shook her head against the leather headrest. "That's too old for this type of bullshit. By then grown people should be tired of playing games!" Carla had spent the better part of the afternoon thinking about her situation and was beyond frustrated that she hadn't been able to reach a conclusion one way or the other.

"I keep forgetting you're so young," Ezekiel said, deciding to respond only to a portion of what she'd said. He actually couldn't recall Carla's exact age. He knew she was at least twenty-one, because she always had to show her identification when they went out. If what she just said was any indication, she wasn't yet twenty-five, though. She was somewhere in between. *Young.* She was still at that idealistic age when the present looks especially rosy and the future is too far away to be taken seriously, but Carla's thoughts were dark and mundane. She was too young for her thoughts. *Too young for you as well,* he added ruefully. He'd counted thirty-three candles on his last birthday cake.

Carla turned in her seat to face him. "What are you going to do about you and Betty Jean?" She hated saying Betty Jean's name, but she'd told herself that she was going to stop tripping on her nemesis so hard. Hated enemy or not, it wasn't her fault that her parents had a little too much imagination, *or not enough of it,* to name her Betty Jean. She damn sure couldn't help it that her man came home to her every night. He was her man, after all. Or at least he used to sleep there, used to be her man, used to come home every night, Carla thought and couldn't stop herself from smiling. Yeah, she'd go easy on old Betty Jean. She could afford to be more charitable. Ezekiel's head was on the pillow next to hers at night now. Betty Jean was a used-to-be.

He'd been looking for a way to say he was going over to Betty Jean's without having to hear Carla talk shit and was glad she'd broached the subject first. He tried to sound casual as he said, "I'm going over there when I drop you off at home."

"Oh." Carla shifted in her seat again with her left leg folded beneath her. The elation caused by her catty thoughts of Betty Jean evaporated instantly and she was left feeling deflated. *Damn, I should have known,* she thought bitterly. She was only filling in until Betty Jean took him back. He'd probably call her later that night with some excuse and apologize. And that was only if she was lucky and ranked higher than she had a few months ago when he hadn't bothered to acknowledge her at all. He'd just turned his back and walked away. How she let him talk his way back in was a mystery. *How the hell did he end up staying at her place, anyway?*

One look at Carla's rapidly changing expressions had Ezekiel frowning. *What the fuck was she thinking about that had her face all twisted up like that*? "I'm just going to pick up some more of my stuff. I don't really even want to talk to her. I'm hoping she's either not there or will let me get in and out without any unnecessary drama."

She cut her eyes at him, slightly mollified by his tone. "Is that right?" One corner of her mouth turned up in a seductive smile and she turned to face him, asking seriously, "You're just getting your shit and leaving? In and out, no bullshitting around? No, *we can work this out, BJ*?" The last was asked in a perfect imitation of Ezekiel, before switching back to her regular voice. "None of that bullshit, huh?"

"Man, why are you tripping, Carla? Why the fuck would I be trying to work things out with Betty Jean after what happened?"

"I don't know why you would or wouldn't. You haven't told me what happened between you and your girl to make you leave. You gave me some vague shit about her pissing you off or crossing the line or something, I don't know. You weren't exactly making sense when you showed up at my apartment. I know you didn't tell me shit, though. What happened between the two of you?"

"Why are you tripping?" He could have told her what Betty Jean had done, but he didn't want to. If he did, Carla would use it as ammunition against BJ, if they ever did get back together. Add that to the fact that he didn't want anybody to know his girl had stepped out on him, and it was a sure bet that he wouldn't ever tell a soul what made him leave Betty Jean.

"I'm tripping, as you put it, because I know your sorry ass, Ezekiel. You'll sit here and guarantee me all day long. Reassuring me, telling me how silly I'm being, while looking me right in my eyes lying. You know your tongue is forked. Stop playing!" She hit at his arm playfully, then rubbed her hand down his chest to rest on his thigh. "I just want to know if you're on the up this time or if I'm about to receive some of what I helped you dish out? So, I'm asking you again. You're just getting your shit and leaving? In and out, no bullshitting around, right?" There was so much hope shining in her eyes, he couldn't do anything except agree.

Why not? he asked himself. Carla wasn't out giving what was his away to anybody that asked. Carla hadn't betrayed him. Why was he still thinking about Betty Jean? She'd shown her true colors. He should be going home to Carla, he thought persuasively, and he would be. As soon as he spoke with Betty Jean. *What did this shit she pulled mean? Was she still his girl?* He didn't like the way this whole business had him feeling. He didn't know if he could ever trust her again, but he still cared about her and if she was properly repentant, she might be able to convince him she was sorry for hurting him.

Everything could return to normal.

He'd have to find a way to placate Carla, but he was sure it could be done. Or, hell, he could go home to Carla at night since that was always one of her issues and spend his spare time with Betty Jean until the move to California. He smiled. Entertained by his fantasies, he planned a little further. He could tell Betty Jean they were starting over and should take it slow. That would keep her off his back about his returning to the house. He thought about all the things Betty Jean would do while trying to win him back over to her side and pushed his thoughts away, promising to think it out more clearly later. He glanced at Carla's hopeful face again, assuring her he'd be *home* that night.

When he pulled up to the curb, Carla hesitated to open the door. In a moment of sheer genius he asked her if she wanted to come along for the ride. If she was with him, he'd be even faster, he said. She hesitated for a moment before shaking her head to decline the offer. She climbed from the car, then leaned across the seat to kiss him before he pulled away from the curb.

Ezekiel exhaled loudly. He'd only offered to let Carla come along because he knew she'd say no. He also knew that the gesture would make Carla feel more secure about his motives, but for a moment...*when she hesitated....* He let the thought trail off, glad that she'd gotten out of the car.

**

It was a night of surprises.

Ezekiel's first surprise came when he pulled into the driveway and let himself into an empty house. Betty Jean wasn't there waiting for him like he was certain she would be. On the drive over, he'd been filled with the anticipation of seeing her again and was more than a little bit hurt that she wasn't home to receive him. Granted, he had told her he'd be there by six and it was after 9:30, but still. He frowned. She could have waited. She was usually patient without complaint. He guessed her little rendezvous in California changed a lot of things. Pouting, he decided to get his belongings and leave before she returned. Evidently, seeing him wasn't high on her list.

Ezekiel frowned in contemplation as he walked through the house, packing the things he would take with him to Carla's. Which brought along his second surprise. Wallowing in disappointment over Betty Jean's absence he hadn't noticed nearly the entire house had been boxed, wrapped or put into a carton. It was not until he noticed that his things stood out starkly against the boxed items that he really looked at his surroundings. There were boxes everywhere. Some were sealed and stacked neatly on top of one another, against the walls. Still more were in the middle of the floors, gaping open, waiting to be filled.

Betty Jean was preparing to leave.

She'd had a few things packed before they'd gone out west, but nothing to this extent. He looked around the house, really seeing it. And he felt himself panicking. BJ was leaving.

The third surprise of the evening followed that realization. He didn't want her to go. He didn't want Betty Jean to leave without him. He needed her. The sudden intensity of his emotions gave him pause, but before he had time to consider them, he heard a key turning in the front door and he froze halfway down the steps. He'd been standing on the staircase surveying the house, trying to decide what to do. *Leave her a note asking her to call him or wait for her so they could speak in person?* She walked in, sparing him the decision.

She dropped the bags she was carrying at the entrance and kicked the door closed with her foot. She turned on the living room light, using the switch by the door, and her eyes went automatically towards where he stood on the stairs. Betty Jean put a hand to her chest, closing her eyes. "Oh, thank God! You should have seen me trying to remain calm."

She stooped to pick up her packages and placed them amongst the clutter on the coffee table. "I could see a silhouette on the staircase, but I didn't know what to think. And you were just standing there. I saw your car outside, but —" She stopped speaking, noticing that Ezekiel still hadn't moved.

He just stood watching her. She frowned. "Why were you in the dark?" The light over the stove was shining faintly from the kitchen, but it barely illuminated the far side of the house. The staircase stood in shadows.

"Sorry, I didn't mean to scare you. You scared me, too, when I saw all these boxes and you weren't here when I came in." He descended the stairs as he spoke, crossing over to where she waited. He stopped when he stood close to Betty Jean.

Too close, she thought, smelling his cologne. *Liz for Men.* Carla's scent. Betty Jean shook her head, suddenly annoyed by her attraction to him. Hell, she felt like *she* was doing something wrong. Like she was seeing someone else's man. Insecurity overrode the irritation in her voice when she said, "You were supposed to be here by six. I waited until nearly eight then I had to leave. I needed to get to a few stores before they closed." She was rambling senselessly about the different choices in box tapes, but couldn't seem to stop the flow of words. Ezekiel was staring at her as he'd done on the stairs, but with him standing so close to her, she felt flustered by the directness of his look.

She wore blue jeans and one of his old tee shirts, he noticed, admiring the curve of her behind. Her hair was pulled back into a ponytail and covered with a baseball cap. She looked sexy as hell to him all thrown together in her loose shirt and tight jeans. He didn't have a clue about what she was talking about. His gaze, along with all his attention, was focused on her mouth. He was leaning over kissing her, before he knew what he was about. He pulled away from her briefly. The kiss had surprised them both. He knew she wasn't offended by his actions though, when he pulled her close for a second kiss and her mouth opened beneath his in a soft sigh of desire. He grabbed her tightly, wanting to taste her better.

Another surprise. Betty Jean was just as hungry for him, because in a flash they were on one another, twisted among the bubble wrap and newspaper. They dug and chewed and clawed each other in a desperate attempt to join flesh and mind and soul. Clothes disappeared and with no conscious thought to do so, Ezekiel drove himself inside of her, digging deeper and deeper. He hammered the entrance to her body, determined that she would know to whom she belonged.

She didn't require the reminder. Betty Jean knew who mastered her fate and captained her soul as she raised her legs higher, bending her knees to allow him further penetration. She raised her hips, spreading her knees further. Opening herself to him. She trembled, shaking from the force of their lovemaking, climaxing again and again. When Ezekiel lay spent and throbbing inside her, her flesh convulsed once again and they lay in a tangle of limbs, sweat and heavy breathing.

**

They'd lain holding one another for a long time before they found the strength to rise. She looked at Ezekiel, then ducked her head blushing over what they'd shared. It was...she searched for the words, but her mind failed her. Never had she felt so much power in their lovemaking. It was literally beyond description.

Her body felt like liquid gold. All melted down and ready to pour. She hated getting up, but they couldn't lie on the living room floor all night. Personally she wouldn't mind, but she'd prefer the king-sized bed upstairs. Ezekiel, she knew, could sleep anywhere. He would be content to sleep right there beside the couch. She stood, stretching back into Ezekiel's tee shirt.

He stood, cupping her behind. Bending slightly, he kissed her neck. Betty Jean leaned into his embrace, sighing. Ezekiel loved her and everything was going to be fine. She closed her eyes, squeezing him tight.

"I'm hungry," she said, looking up at him, smiling. "I haven't had a chance to eat all day." She turned towards the stairs. "Let me take a quick shower, then I'll come back and fix us something. Are you hungry?" The question was lost in a muffle of fabric as she removed the tee shirt for the second time that night, sprinting quickly up the steps. She felt rejuvenated.

Ezekiel reached for his clothes. Damn, it felt so good holding Betty Jean. She always got so wet. He smiled arrogantly. California boy hadn't changed that. Whatever he'd done hadn't affected her response to him. Dude probably didn't even know she could get that hot. She hadn't wanted him like she wanted Zeke. She only had sex with dude out of anger. Ezekiel zipped his pants up then reconsidered and stepped into the half bath beneath the staircase to wash. The last thing he needed was to give Carla something to bitch about. He glanced at his watch, cursing. She was already going to bitch. He'd been gone way longer than the time it takes to pack the few things he was returning to Carla's with. He finished cleaning up and dressing then headed for the stairs. He didn't have time to eat, but after what just took place between them he was definitely going to give more thought to moving back home.

She was humming softly to herself in the shower when he tapped at the door, letting himself into the bathroom. "Hey, I have to go. It's later than I thought, okay?" He raised his voice to be heard over her own and the running water.

The singing stopped abruptly.

Betty Jean stuck her head out between the shower curtain and the wall. "What? I didn't hear you." Water ran from her hair down the side of her face and she wiped it away with a soapy hand.

"I'm going to head out. I'll have to catch you later on something to eat."

Betty Jean stared at him incredulously for a long moment before pulling her head back into the shower. *I'll have to catch you later....* His words floated through her mind again and again, repeating themselves.

"I'll see you later," he called as he closed the bathroom door. He'd told Carla he'd be right back and his time was up. She'd be blowing him up on his cell phone pretty soon and he'd rather avoid that bullshit if he could. That was another point in Betty Jean's favor. She never demanded anything of him. He smiled a little to himself. He had it good with Betty Jean, even he had to admit that. She wasn't the mouthy type. He didn't have to worry about catching drama from her.

He thought about the time she'd left him. Packed and moved without an explanation. To this very day, he still didn't know why she'd left. She refused all questions. His thoughts progressed to the mysterious man in California and he scowled a bit. Betty Jean wasn't a *sayer*. She was a doer. Instead of cussing and fussing at him about his behavior like Carla might do, Betty Jean would devise a plan and act on it. But even so, her drama queen ratio was still really low.

He picked up the gym bag he'd filled with another week's worth of things and walked from the bedroom. When he reached the landing, he looked back over his shoulder towards the room. Part of him wanted to strip down and join Betty Jean in the shower, but he had to go back to Carla's. At least for tonight. He'd think up something to remedy the situation during the next few days. *Soon he'd be back home with his baby,* he thought smiling. Damn, it felt good to have Betty Jean all over him like that again.

He was midway down the staircase before he received his next surprise. Without warning, a wet Betty Jean leapt onto his back pounding his head and shoulders with her fists. By some miracle he was able to keep his balance and remain upright with her added weight on his back.

Unfortunately, when she jumped on his back his hand released his gym bag and it tumbled down the remaining stairs ahead of him, landing right where his foot would find it. When he felt them being propelled forward he tried to step over the bag, but stumbled across it instead as he and Betty Jean careened in a drunken whirlwind across the foyer and into the living room.

He tried in vain to dislodge Betty Jean from his back, but couldn't.

She was still wet from her shower and he couldn't get a firm hold on her. She, however, had a rather tenacious grip on him as she continued to pummel him. Finally, Ezekiel fell back against the couch with Betty Jean behind and beneath him on the cushion. She was the shell on his turtle, as he struggled to rise.

Dodging her swinging fists, he pried her legs from around his body. He tried to stand up quickly, but she snagged a handful of his shirt collar and wouldn't let go. He was coughing and choking. She was screaming incoherently. Or at least, whatever she was saying was indecipherable for him. Ezekiel's own thoughts were too muddled from Betty Jean's sudden and wholly unexpected attack to think straight. He was beyond comprehending anything being said at the moment. His collar was cutting off his oxygen and spots danced before his eyes. Later he would recall cursing and fighting his way to the door, his shirt hanging torn and crooked off one shoulder.

He pulled fiercely. There was a loud rent in the air, as his shirt finally gave way and he tore himself from her grasp. Betty Jean kept coming towards him, though, attacking in all her naked glory and he kept pushing her back. Somehow he collected his bag from where it had been kicked against the door and got out of the house.

But more surprises were to come as a naked Betty Jean followed him outside.

Ezekiel hurried across the lawn to his car.

He looked back over his shoulder, fumbling with his keys and Betty Jean was there on the porch. She was searching the area around her. He threw his belongings into the car. Jamming the key into the ignition he started the engine. He was shifting into reverse just as she was straightening up, having found what she sought. He was screeching out the driveway when the rock she'd thrown smashed against the hood with a loud bang, barely missing the front windshield. Absurdly, later he would recall thinking she had a pretty good arm.

**

Carla was watching television when he knocked. She looked at the front door, picked up the remote and flipped through the channels. She was lighting an incense stick from the red glow of a philly blunt, when the door opened and Ezekiel walked in, dropping his bag at the door.

"Why didn't you say something when you unlocked the door? I was just supposed to keep standing outside?" he grumbled, taking off the remnants of his shirt. Wadding it into a ball, he threw it onto the gym bag he'd dropped by the door.

Carla blew smoke to the ceiling, cutting her eyes at him sideways. "Because I never locked the door. I took a long bath when I got home, so I left it unlocked. I didn't want you to be locked out or have to get out of the tub. You know, since you were coming right back?"

Her polite tone was the embodiment of sarcasm and Ezekiel sucked his teeth. He did not need this shit. Not right now. His back and head were still aching like hell. And his throat felt like it was twice its normal size. There was no way in hell he was going to listen to Carla's bullshit after just having had to deal with Betty Jean's crazy ass.

Damn, he couldn't believe she'd jumped on his back like that. Fucking crazy ass bitch. She could have killed them both. He rubbed at his neck and shoulders, feeling stiffness setting in, and he rotated his joints. Shit, maybe that was her intention. If her motive hadn't been to kill herself, she was damn sure trying to do him in.

"I'm sorry." He rubbed his hands down his face, removing his glasses. He would apologize to appease Carla's ass, because he could see bullshit brewing, then he was going to bed. "I didn't mean to be gone so long. It was a three-ring circus over there. I'm glad you didn't come with me. There's no telling what Crazy would have done."

"Crazy, is she now?" Carla smiled, but without mirth. The sneer she wore was a smudge of contempt when she looked at him. "Why do you men always have to make a girl crazy once she gets tired of your shit and starts responding to your dumb asses in kind? As long as she's putting up with whatever bit of nonsense you're feeding her, everything's fine. She's still who-the-fuck-ever, being a good girl. Once she finds her fucking backbone and stands up for herself, she's Crazy."

Carla turned away from him, flipping through more channels. It wasn't that she was trying to defend Betty Jean, she wasn't. She was just trying to clarify something that had always puzzled her. If you ask a man what happened between him and his ex, nine times out of ten, he was going to say they broke up because she was crazy. Carla took a drag from the philly. Glancing at Ezekiel she pulled a face. She knew one day she'd be crazy by his definition, too. She shook her head. She didn't even want to know what Thom said about her. Probably, that she was certifiable.

Irritated that he'd been demanding of her attention more and more lately, she gave the cigar another hard pull, holding the smoke until her eyes burned. Thomas's dark handsome face came to her clearly and she allowed him to linger there a moment, before blowing him away in a puff of smoke. *Too bad Ezekiel doesn't smoke,* she thought, observing him closely again. *He sure looks like he could use a toke or two.* The notion of Ezekiel smoking was so preposterous it caused her lips to curl in a brief smile.

Seeing the smile, Ezekiel frowned deeply. Misreading the reasons behind it, he said, "This shit is not funny. She almost killed me. I'm calling Betty Jean's ass Crazy because her *crazy* ass attacked me!" He stressed the second crazy in his sentence, gaining Carla's interest as he circled around to sit in one of the chairs. He threw his head back against the cushion. "I still can't believe she acted like that." He shook his head in genuine disbelief. "I'm walking down the stairs with my shit, about to leave, right? And out of nowhere, this broad jumps on my back and starts beating the shit out of me! No explanation. No nothing. She just starts swinging."

A smile stretched across Carla's lips. "And that's how it happened, your honor," she said in a solemn voice, raising her right hand as if to be pledged in.

"Fuck you, Carla, okay?"

They were silent for a moment, but Carla's curiosity had been piqued and she prodded him for further details. "No shit? Miss I've Got a College Education was playing Kermit and did a leap frog onto your back?" Without waiting for an answer, she fell back against the couch laughing. Her laughter turned to strong coughing and she placed the blunt in the ashtray.

Zeke closed his eyes, shaking his head in disbelief. Betty Jean. Standing outside, ass out, throwing rocks! He didn't know what the hell was wrong with her. He didn't even know she could act like that. She'd never been in a ghetto a day in her life, but she'd gone there quick enough. Went straight to it, like she'd been born and raised to act like that. Hell, he wasn't even sure about the acting "ghetto" analogy. He'd dated some project girls that wouldn't do what BJ had done. No telling how many of their neighbors were watching through their windows, witnessing her naked ass act a fool.

"That's what took you so long to get back? Your mad dash to the door? The struggling and fighting?" Lost in his own reflections, Ezekiel hadn't noticed that Carla stopped laughing. There was something deceptive in the calm of her question that made Ezekiel open his eyes. He didn't trust the change in the atmosphere and reached to put his glasses back on his face.

"Man, I thought I was going to have to swing on her to get out of there. I've never struck a woman in my life, but I can see what will drive a man to do it. Two more seconds and I would have swung, I promise. It was getting crucial over there."

"So, the shit I'm staring at must have happened in the tussle." Carla sat quietly on the edge of the couch watching him.

Inwardly, he cursed. *Shit. Shit. Shit.* He wanted to look down and see what she was looking at, maybe he could come up with something plausible. But to look down would be an admission that something could be there. He already knew he'd been told on. He'd returned with evidence of what he'd been doing with Betty Jean. It was in Carla's tone. She could have said, "You're dick's hanging out" and he wouldn't have been surprised to see it dangling from his pants. He thought hard for a second, replaying his and Betty Jean's time together that night, mentally trying to see what Carla had seen. He'd vividly recalled what he and Betty Jean were up to before she'd gone ballistic. He didn't have to see it with his own eyes to know Betty Jean had left her mark on him. Her stamp of ownership.

As it turned out, he didn't have to do anything. Carla's look said she already knew the answer to her question. When a woman has you dead center and is giving you *the look*, while she uses *the tone*, all that's left to do is tell the truth.

Shit, he hated that look.

He should just tell Carla the truth and be done with it, he thought. But he couldn't do it. He closed his eyes again, suddenly weary. His lashes had barely fallen when they immediately sprang open. He wasn't taking his eyes off a woman when he was unsure of what was in her mind. He wouldn't make that mistake again. Betty Jean's attack was a lesson still too freshly learned. He didn't know what the fuck Carla was sitting there thinking.

He didn't have to wait long to find out.

"That's how you're going to play it, huh? Just flip the script on us two? Now you come home to me after fucking her? I guess I do get some of what I helped dish out. Do I get a kiss after you've licked all over her pussy? Did you ever go home and kiss her with me still dripping from your tongue? She get a taste of me, too, Zeke?" Her voice was deliberately sensuous and he groaned out loud until the sound vibrated from the walls.

Zeke stood from the chair. Marching over to the shirt he'd discarded, he picked it up. Shaking it in his fist, he stretched it out before him. "Did I tear my shirt up before coming inside your apartment? Did I do that shit myself, just so I could come in here and lie to you? I guess in her frenzied passion, she clawed at my neck, too." He bent close so Carla could view the scratches he felt on his throat. The wounds acquired in his battle to get to the door.

Carla hesitated, trying to decide if she was going to believe *him* or what her eyes could see. It was apparent that something physical had occurred between the two of them. *Could the small, dime-sized circle she'd seen be just another bruise?* He *was* all scratched and marked up. She took in Ezekiel's appearance and reluctantly applauded her arch rival. The true source of that particular mark may be in question, but Carla had no doubts that even if he got some pussy, he'd gotten his ass kicked, too.

Their evening may have started out sweet, but it sure as hell ended on a sour note. It was clear that Betty Jean had put her hands all over Ezekiel and a small little piece of Carla was thrilled by the prospect. *Bet he felt like he was in church*, she thought unkindly, remembering how her mother's church always ended with the laying on of hands. She gave him a long, hard assessment before turning her head back to the television set, deciding to let the matter drop. From the looks of him, she doubted he'd be going back to Betty Jean's any time soon. He was dismissed from her mind as she retrieved what remained of her blunt, searching the couch for her lighter.

Fourteen

She laughed into the phone. "Yes, I did, girl! No, I didn't put anything on first. He would have gotten away!" Her laughter mingled with Sheila's on the other end of the line and she was glad. Confiding in Sheila that day at the office had been one of her better decisions. It felt good to have someone to talk to. Unburdening herself was therapeutic.

She'd wanted to call Saturday night as soon as she'd stormed back into the house, but she needed to cool off first. She was happy she'd waited. Saturday night when she attacked Ezekiel she couldn't ever remember being that angry. For the first time in her life, she'd reached her pisstifity. When she was younger she'd heard her mother and her friends saying how someone had *pissed them off to their highest pisstifity*, but she'd never actually thought it was real.

In her youthful, carefree mind, she figured it was just a silly word someone made up. *Pisstifity.* Doesn't even sound real. After last night, her skepticism was a thing of the past. She now knew that the mythical level of anger truly did exist. *Pisstifity*. The highest point of anger that can be reached without committing a felony. That was the definition given to her a long time ago, when she still lived in doubt.

Yes, she was glad she'd waited before calling Sheila. In the bright light of a Sunday morning spent in bed, she could see the humor in her actions. Saturday night she was not in a laughing mood. "Hell, I just snapped. He was trying to reduce me to one of his little hoes, as though he'd lost his mind. When he first said he was about to leave, I was going to accept it. I pulled my head back in the shower disgusted with myself for being such a damn fool. It hadn't taken him any effort at all to get my panties down. I just fell down at his feet like a little lap dog, glad he was home. The longer I thought about it, the more pissed off I got. More at myself than at him, but I didn't have any problem channeling my hostility, you know? I can whup his ass better than I can my own, right? My only focus was doing just that and I tried. I tried hard. I know he thinks I'm crazy, but I'm not. For that moment, I was certifiably insane and he'd better recognize the fucking difference."

"What's the difference?" Sheila inquired from the other end of the phone, laughing at a cursing Betty Jean. "Just so I'll be able to tell them apart, as well." She was delighted in Betty Jean's bravado. Sheila hoped she left marks on him that he'd be busy trying to explain for the next week. Like a black eye or a chipped tooth.

"Aunt Gertrude who talks to her handbag and thinks her Sunday coat can convey messages to the dead is crazy."

"You have an Aunt Gertrude that talks to her handbag?"

"*Everyone* has an Aunt Gertrude who talks to her handbag," Betty Jean replied, dryly. "When the serial killer's neighbors are interviewed on television they never say *I always knew something was wrong.* They say, *He was such a sweet man, blah, blah, blah. Never would have suspected, blah, blah, blah. I still can't believe, blah, blah, blah.* That's because he was *insane*. Had his ass been crazy everybody would have known about it. Crazy people stand out. The insane know how to blend in with society. The insane are way more dangerous. No one knows we're a few sandwiches shy of a good picnic until it's too damned late to do anything about it."

"And you're certain which category you fit into?" Sheila joked. "How easily are you blending in right about now, Streaker? Sure you aren't just crazy?"

Betty Jean got a flash of herself standing on the porch of her house naked as the day she was born, throwing rocks and cursing and she laughed again, before saying seriously, "Girl, a man will make you forget every ounce of education you ever had, okay? All common sense is gone, too. He will make you act a fool until you're so far removed from who you are you need a road map just to find your way back and a goddamned introduction to yourself when you get there."

Betty Jean sat up suddenly in the bed. Sitting up straight, she squared her shoulders. Looking around the half-packed bedroom, she introduced herself to an imaginary group of strangers. "Hello, I'm Betty Jean Carlson and I've been a fool." She ran a hand through her disheveled hair. "I feel like I need a twelve step program. Maybe JA — Jackass Anonymous."

Betty Jean fell back against the pillows, pulling the covers over her head. She lay there for a moment pondering her circumstance, then threw the covers back. Damned if she was going to spend the day lying around feeling sorry for herself. Okay, she took a blow to her spirit last night, but Ezekiel took a blow everywhere else!

She swung her legs over the side of the bed saying, "I *am* Betty Jean Carlson, Sheila, and it's about time I started acting like it!" She stood from the bed, stretching. "Girl, I've got things to do. People to see!" She felt suddenly energized. "Nothing and no one, specifically.

It just sounds good," she said, answering Sheila's question of what she had to do. "I may hit the mall later. If you want to come along I'll give you a call." Betty Jean stepped into the bathroom as she hung up, closing the door behind her.

**

Sheila stuck her head through the opening she'd made in the door. "You have a call on line one, Streaker."

Betty Jean smiled. "That gets less funny every time you say it," she said, referring to the moniker Sheila had given her after her confession on Sunday; she didn't want it overheard. It was a private joke she didn't want people wondering and asking about. Instead of buzzing Betty Jean on the intercom, she'd been getting up from her desk all morning whenever she felt like saying it. And she felt like saying it often.

"No, it doesn't, because I'm still willing to get up out of my seat just to say it," Sheila countered, closing the door before Betty Jean could respond again.

Betty Jean shook her head laughing. She never got the last word with her assistant. "Betty Jean Carlson, may I help you?" she asked, rapidly into the telephone, as she continued to type.

The voice that said hello was familiar, but she couldn't place it. She typed on, impatient to hang up. She didn't have time for lengthy discussions. She had too many things to do. It was the caller's next words that finally stilled her fingers.

"You're a difficult lady to find, Bee."

Bee.

Her eyes widened and she was thankful for her head set. She would have dropped the phone had she been holding it. There were only two people who called her Bee and she was positive it couldn't be her mother's voice in her ear. She touched a finger to the earpiece of her head set, pressing it closer for clarity. "Who is this?" Her eyes narrowed in suspicion.

"I'll only tell you if you promise you won't be upset with me for contacting you."

The voice was a rich baritone that curled her toes in her shoes and had her whispering, "Byron?"

"Hello, Queen Bee," he repeated his greeting. "Don't start yelling at me, all right? I know you have a man. I'm not trying to crack you up or anything –"

"Crack me up?" she interrupted, asking.

"Yeah, crack the two of you up. Break you up. Split you up. You know."

"I'm sorry for interrupting." Betty Jean tried not to laugh. "I'd just never heard the expression before. Well, not used like that, I haven't."

"It's all the same thing. Crack. Break. Split. Divide. I just choose to use the less familiar term," Byron explained his quirk, fascinated by the turn in conversation.

"What you're saying isn't correct, though."

"Why not?" he asked intrigued. He liked her better each time her spoke to her. They could talk about anything, it seemed, and make it entertaining.

"To crack something is to do just that. To crack it. A crack is not a break, split or division. With either of those three a whole piece becomes two or more. When there's a crack in something, it's still one piece, just damaged. Sometimes repairable, sometimes not."

"You sure?"

"Yeah, pretty much," she said, enjoying the banter.

He was quiet for a moment as if considering what she said. "I like crack up better than break up. Everyone says break up. I like to stand out." He sounded disappointed, then brightened. "I'm going to use it anyway." His voice held such petulance, they both laughed.

"You're just making up your own little dialect," she said it as more of a statement than a question and Byron stepped back into his explanation regarding his call.

"I'm not trying to step between you and your man, but I've got you stuck in my head, Bee. I thought maybe if I spoke to you I could shake you loose, but I can already tell that it didn't work." Now that he had her on the phone the prospect of ridding her from his mind seemed more unlikely. He only wanted to see her more. She was just as intriguing to him as she'd been a week ago. His desire to see her and spend time with her intensified and he offered to take her to lunch.

"Aren't you in California?" Betty Jean asked, surprised and a little excited. She was only vaguely aware that she was hoping he was nearby.

"Yes, but I can fly down to have lunch with you and fly home again after we eat."

"Okay, *after we eat*," she repeatedly dubiously.

Byron laughed into the phone, picking up her thoughts. "Is that all you think about?" He laughed again, cutting off her protest. "Seriously, Queen Bee. I know we jumped ahead the night we met. I know you were going through something, hurting some, and you used me to heal yourself a little bit."

On her end of the line, Betty Jean was dead silent. He was right. She had used him, because of Zeke. She'd been in more than *some* pain that night, though. She'd been in desperate need, she was hurting so bad. She felt like a heartless witch that he knew it, though. That he knew she was with him because of what she was letting someone else put her through emotionally. She felt even worse because he said *used*. She did use him, but still.... He didn't have to put it out there like that.

"I knew that night you weren't the type of woman to take a strange man to your bed. That casual sex just wasn't something you did. When you were telling me about your man at the restaurant, I figured he must have busted you up pretty badly. You were putting up a brave front, but you were hurting."

"So, did you take advantage?" Betty Jean asked softly into the phone. She was so affected by his words, she didn't even comment on his usage of busted. It was enough that she understood how he meant it.

"Hell, yes!" Byron said. His honesty allowed Betty Jean to relax. "A better man would have left you alone, not wanting you to regret anything that happened. But I would have regretted it had I walked away from you. It would have been something else if you were married. I would have just seen you back to your room and left. I try to avoid that sort of madness. I don't usually deal with a woman who's living with someone, either, but I liked you. And you weren't wearing a ring. And you only referred to him as your man, not your husband. Anyway, I'm just saying that I'd like to see you, again," he said, bringing the conversation back to lunch. "I don't think I'm so grotesque that I have to fly to another state to get some loving. Of course, as good as we were, I'd gladly hop a flight for it, but right now I'll settle for just seeing you and spending some time in your company."

"Don't you have to go to work? Aren't you at work?" she amended, thinking of the time difference in California. He was two hours behind her. The middle of the day.

"I work nights mostly. There's not much to do in the daytime."

"What kind of work do you do?" Betty Jean asked. They'd talked about a lot of things that night, but she couldn't recall him speaking of his occupation. He'd told her of the years he modeled and some of the people he'd met and worked with, but they hadn't discussed the present much.

"I work at Rufio's."

"Yes, that's right! You were out scouting the line. I'd forgotten, just that quick. Wait! If you were working at Rufio's why did you just leave with me? You didn't get in any trouble for leaving, did you? Especially since it was so close to the end of the night?" Because she'd monopolized his time that night, once they entered the club, she'd forgotten he'd been working when she originally saw him. He hadn't informed anyone when they left, either. At least not that she noticed. They just got up from the table and walked out the door.

"No, no one said anything to me about leaving. My presence there is no big deal. But we weren't near closing time. Rufio's stays open twelve hours. Five-to-five. It's always crowded, too, even after we stop selling drinks."

He didn't say it, but the pride in his tone made her ask, "What exactly do you do at Rufio's?"

"There's not much I haven't done there. I've actually worked every position. I've done it all." His tone was evasive, but she could hear the amusement, as well. Byron owned Rufio's, but it was something he didn't mention unless it was necessary. Too many women were attracted to the owner of the hottest club in the city and not the man. Just his bank statement. He was accustomed to people seeing dollar signs when they looked at him, but still he learned to pocket his ownership until he knew his audience better.

"Please don't tell me. I'm worried about you getting in trouble with yourself, aren't I? You're the head manager."

"No, I'm not the head manager. Rufio's doesn't have a head manager. Are you going to let me take you to lunch or not?"

He'd switched subjects. Betty Jean recalled the night they'd spent together and realized he'd done the same thing then. Whenever the question came up of his current circumstances, he'd tell her a story of what he once did. She'd allow him his mystery and wouldn't ask again about his employment. She wasn't trying to get to know him, anyway. But there was one thing she'd like to know and asked, "How'd you get my work number?"

She could feel him smile into the phone. "That's confidential information, Queen Bee. I could tell you, but then I'd have to kill you."

"Is it as cloak and dagger as all that?" She tried to sound bored but the words came out sultry instead. She frowned. *Was she crazy?* She did not need this complication. She was on the phone flirting with another man when she didn't know what to do with the one she had. If she still had him, she amended. Her attack had been pretty brutal.

"No, but it's a story better told over a dinner table with wine and music, than a telephone. It'll lose the ambiance in the telling having to travel through wire."

Betty Jean laughed in spite of herself. She couldn't help it. Byron had charm and apparently, he wasn't above using it to get his way. She couldn't remember the last time she'd been openly pursued to such a degree and the attention felt nice. Flattering. She wondered if he simply remembered her company's name from their dinner conversation. It would have been easy from that point. Once you got the company's phone number, there was an office directory that would lead you straight to the person you were seeking. She only asked him how he did it to see if she'd guessed correctly, but he wanted it to sound like he contacted the NSA or something, so she'd let him keep his little secret for now.

She wondered if he recalled her telling him of her move to the West Coast. It was quick to find her this time, but in a few days, searching for her would be a *Where's Waldo* poster. Unless he remembered Hurstwode & Donovan, she'd be lost to him again. It was a shame, too, she thought. He seemed like a nice enough guy.

She told him her thoughts as they were hanging up the phone and he propositioned her. "Say you'll have lunch with me when I find you again."

Betty Jean hesitated. "Why should I?"

"Why should you say it or why should you do it?"

"Surprise me."

"I thought I had already," he shot back, smiling into the phone. Man, he would love the chance to get to know this woman. "Come on, cut me a break, since you haven't given me one yet. Come on," he coaxed, further. "Agree to go out with me when I find you on the coast, Queen Bee."

Feeling reckless, she agreed. *What harm could come of it?* Sure, she'd been easy to find somewhere she'd been established for years, but out west it wouldn't be so simple. But on the off chance that he did find her, she'd be true to her word and have lunch with him. He'd have to find her first, though. The thought of him searching for her put butterflies in her stomach and she chided herself, she was too old for butterflies. She'd barely disconnected the call when Sheila burst into the office seeking details.

**

Tuesday morning Carla woke with a feeling of dread. Something was wrong, but she didn't know what. Something other than the fact that it was just past three in the morning and she was suddenly wide awake and apprehensive.

She got out of bed careful not to wake Ezekiel and went into the living room. She turned on the lamp, then turned the knob, dimming the light. Pacing back and forth, she circled the room three times before forcing herself to sit down. Her uneasiness was growing and she still didn't know the cause of it. She noticed her book *Too Deep for Tears* tucked in between the couch cushions and reached for it. Finding her mark, she read aloud softly.

like a bird
spread my wings
off towards freedom
and distant things

sunshine beneath my spread
freedom from the worries
inside my head
blessed Heaven
above and beneath
so high up
out of Life's reach
no mountains to conquer
no point to prove
no having to dance
to Destiny's groove
just up and above
gone and away
nothing to do
nothing clever to say
just give me wings
so i may fly
chained to this earth
my spirit dies
hear my prayer
my heartfelt plea
give me wings
so i'll be free

She sat quietly, thinking of the words in the poem. *Would she ever know true freedom? What was true freedom?* Carla placed her finger in the book to hold her spot, then flipped it over, looking at the spine. She'd never heard of the author before. It was the woman's first poetry publication, but whoever she was, Carla understood what she had to say and thought that the book was aptly titled. *Too Deep for Tears*, indeed. *What part of life wasn't?* When the phone rang, she jumped. With her heart beating out a ragged tattoo, she ran to the phone. Half afraid to say anything, she breathed, "Hello," into the receiver.

The voice that responded whispered as well. It too was leery of what the early morning hours had in store.

"Hey, I'm sorry to wake you, but there wasn't too much I could do about it." There was a pause before he hurried on, "My car is parked in front of your place. The keys are under your welcome mat."

"Why?" she broke in, confused.

"I didn't want to leave you and my little Ebony doll without transportation. There's also about six hundred dollars in an envelope in the glove compartment. Try not to let that sit in there too long, okay? When we hang up go get it, all right? Or get it first thing in the morning. It's not much, but it's all I had in my savings account and I'm not trying to give it to no crack-head. Put it up somewhere safe for you and Ebony. You need to open a bank account or something, really. Stop wasting your money at those check cashing places." He spoke rapidly, as though there weren't enough time to say everything that needed said. "Hurry up and get the keys from under your mat, too. That shit ain't safe."

"Thomas, you're scaring the shit out of me. Why are you giving me your money? Why is your car outside my house?" She peeked through the curtains in the living room, confirming his words. Sure enough, his car was parked downstairs. "What do you mean, you didn't want to leave us without transportation?"

"I'm leaving in less than an hour. I enlisted, Carla."

"Enlisted in what?" She tried to calm herself, but it was proving hard. *What the fuck did he mean he enlisted?* There was only one kind of enlisted that she knew and there was no way in hell Thomas had done that. He couldn't have. He would not have committed himself to such a thing without discussing it with her first. This was a dream. A goddamned nightmare.

"The Air Force. I'd been thinking about it for a while, trying to find a way to survive these streets. I need a real job, with some real money. A fucking skill, some training. Something. Anything, shit. I can't keep living from day to day, barely making it. This can't be my life, Carla."

"You think going into the military is going to get you paid? They don't earn shit. They expect you to pledge your life for a little piece of nothing every month. I probably make more than a motherfucker in boot camp makes and you know what my checks look like. That's without the benefit of having anybody shooting at me, too. This is fucking crazy." Her anger made her curse at Thom. She couldn't believe she was having this conversation at 3:30 in the morning. She couldn't believe he'd done this without talking to her. If she had more time she could change his mind. She could make him see what he was doing was stupid.

"I wanted to talk to you about this the other day when I came by your place." There was a pause as he thought about what he wanted to say. "I could be like the recruiter and tell you all the benefits of me going into the Air Force, but I won't bullshit you, C. Even if I tried to shit you, you'd know it and call me on it. I signed up for the service because I love you with my whole heart and I can't sit around and watch you live your life with someone else. I've been thinking about my own future for a long time and what to do about it. I started talking to the recruiter months ago. I tried to talk to you, but you wouldn't let me. You know how you can be sometimes." There was no accusation in his words, just truth. "I can talk and talk and you'll just imitate a brick wall. Cold and silent."

She said nothing, because she knew she was guilty. The last few times she'd seen Thomas she could tell he had something on his mind, something to say, and each time she was relieved that he hadn't been able to get it said. She couldn't fault him for finally reaching a decision without her input.

"I figured I couldn't sit around forever waiting. Especially if it was someone else you wanted."

"You're not waiting any more?" Carla whispered softly into the phone, not trusting her voice. *I'll kill all that noise*, she heard him saying again. There was a lump in her throat she could barely swallow around and she felt weak. *Really, really weak,* she thought as she sat down heavily at the kitchen table.

"I'll always be right here for you, Carla," he said and his voice shook slightly. "For both my girls, but this is something I have to do." He held the phone for a second, listening to her silence. He closed his eyes, shaking his head. She was always silent when he needed her to say something. Anything. He waited a moment longer, before saying, "I love you girl. Take care of my baby. I'll write you as soon as I can. And Carla," he waited for her response, then said, "take care of yourself. Don't let some busta come along and mess you up. Look, I have to go, baby. You be good. Or at least make it look like you tried," he teased. "I love you."

She barely had time to respond before he was gone. The dial tone replaced his voice.

**

"You look scary. What's wrong?" Monica placed her hand on Carla's shoulder, squeezing gently. She had faint circles beneath her eyes and was much too quiet. The poor girl had been dragging around all day and Monica simply couldn't take it anymore. She'd finally cornered her when Carla went down to the stockroom in the basement to check the store's inventory.

Carla was still too freshly wounded to play coy and pretend not to know what Monica was talking about. She would bet she did look scary. She felt like she was shuffling through thick mud. "Thomas left. He just left, Monica." She looked at her friend with eyes so filled with sadness Monica nearly cried herself. Carla told her about waking in the early morning hours with an uneasy feeling and Thomas's phone call. "I can't believe he left," she repeated for the third time. "I keep trying to wrap my mind around the whole idea, but I can't. I feel like – I feel like this is all a dream. A bad dream at that." She held out her arm. "Please pinch me. Wake me the fuck up."

Monica shook her head in sympathy, rubbing the offered limb. "You didn't have any idea he was going to do something like this?"

Thomas's visit from Friday replayed in her mind, but Carla shook it away. She didn't want to examine it too closely. If she did, she'd have to admit that Thomas had given her a chance to say how she felt. A chance to stop him, but she'd opted for silence. Even in the wee hours of the morning, he had paused, waiting for her to say something, but even then, she couldn't get the words past her lips. Carla stared down at the floor. "Thom has always taken care of me. Not always just with money, either, you know? He just took care of me," she said, hunching her shoulders in understated misery. "I'm kind of scared to think about his not being here." Tears fell from her eyes and she wiped at them with the back of her hand.

Monica hugged her close. "Child, you'll be fine. You and that sweet little girl of yours. This is the time for you to think about your own future and get *you* together while he works on himself."

Carla smiled, straightening away from her friend. She dabbed at her eyes with her fingertips. "I can't believe you'd use a time like this as an opportunity to peddle your college wares to me."

Monica wiped at her own moist eyes, flashing her signature smile. "You have to admit, it was a perfect opening. Now come on, give me half of that inventory list and start talking."

Carla gave two of the five sheets she held to Monica and searched for a place to begin her tale. Shrugging her shoulders, she decided to start at the beginning. The night she and Thomas ended. For the first time ever, she spoke of what Thomas had done. She told the story in a detached voice as though the experience belonged to someone else and not herself.

Monica was mildly surprised by the telling of the story. She'd met Carla's Thom a number of times over the years and although he tried to hide it, it was always obvious how much he cared about Carla. She had thought it was a shame that they weren't together anymore. Especially when they brought Ebony in for ice cream sometimes. They were so cute together, the three of them. They were a family and Monica wished they could live as one. Now that she knew the reason behind their split up, she felt even sorrier for them. It was sad how a bad decision or a moment of anger could destroy something in an instant that had taken years to build.

"You never forgave him," she said the thought aloud, causing Carla to look her way.

"I'm not sure what I did, other than get really goddamned angry. I didn't come from the greatest of families, you know. Someone was always getting stitched up around my house, until it wasn't even a big deal anymore." She lifted her shoulders, shrugging off a past she couldn't change and didn't like thinking about, then let them fall.

She smiled weakly. It only pulled at one corner of her mouth. "It wasn't the old man, either. I mean, pops had a temper, too, but it didn't have shit on my mama's. The old man kept his temper and all the fucked up shit he did strictly for mama, like it was just her he hated, but she didn't discriminate. She had no problem sharing the love. When she was mad, she would strike out at anybody unfortunate enough to be around at the moment. It didn't matter who it was."

Carla's eyes rested on Monica's face, but they didn't see her. They were focused on a childhood she'd never spoken of to anyone. Except Thom, who already knew. He'd been there. "I wrote this speech for Black history month when I was in school that I was selected to read at the school assembly. I never read it. My old man went out on Friday night and didn't come back until Sunday afternoon. We all knew what that would mean.

Mama was going to be in a mood and it would be best to avoid her."

Carla stopped talking to count an open sleeve of cups and Monica prompted softly, "You couldn't avoid her."

Carla shook her head and the words on her inventory sheet blurred. She cleared her throat, saying without emotion, "Nope. Didn't get a chance. I just happened to be in the living room when he came home. Couldn't get my shit up and get out of the house fast enough," she said, shrugging away the memory. "I couldn't go back to school until Thursday. She'd struck my face a couple of times and there wasn't shit I could do to hide the marks. There was no way in hell I was getting up in front of that assembly with my face all tri-colored." She shook her head at the memory of the beating. "Man, fuck that assembly, I wasn't even going to school, shit. Thomas skipped with me for three days, so I wouldn't be lonely and bored. We hung out at this game room downtown," she said absently with a smile for the recollection. "He was like that. Always looking out for me. Always there. That's why I was so hurt by what he did. Hell, wasn't no point in him being there for me and having my back if he was just going to replace my mama later, you know?"

Monica looked at Carla's bowed head in understanding. She'd never been able to forgive Thomas for becoming what he once tried to protect her from. Monica could see the logic behind it, but she could see Carla's sorrow, as well.

"Do you still love him?"

"I buried my feelings for Thomas a long time ago."

"Try answering again, without pride dictating your words." Carla opened her mouth, then closed it. She stood staring down at the clipboard in her hand, picking at a faded sticker. Frowning, she opened her mouth again to speak. Again, she closed it. Monica nodded her head in confirmation. "See there? You don't know what you feel. You buried your feelings for him, but you may want to check and be certain they're dead. Take it from an old wise woman: pride is not your friend. Pride is a good companion to lean on when you need a little strength. You can feel it put steel in your spine, when you feel like crawling around on the floor. But pride is too greedy to keep around for too long, it doesn't know when to stop. It'll put steel in your spine, yes, then all around and inside you until everything's hard as a rock. It's not satisfied until it's consumed everything and it's all you have left. I know you've heard people say, *I've still got my pride.* Pay attention and look and see what else they have. Nothing. Pride has cleaned them out and left them empty-handed."

Carla's frown deepened. *Was pride the reason she never forgave Thomas?* No, she thought stubbornly, barely giving the idea purchase. She never forgave him because.... She searched her mind and could think of nothing. The night he raised his hand to her was the only ill he'd ever done her, but she'd closed up and walked away like it was the last straw in years filled with nothing but hay. The pride that kept her upright for so many years in her parents' house had hardened her heart to any thoughts of forgiveness. She placed him on her list of enemies at the moment of transgression and left him there. Never allowing herself to look too closely to see if he deserved to be exiled.

Now he was gone from her and it no longer mattered. She felt the loss of Thomas keenly. The realization that Thomas was gone snuck up and attacked her in such a fashion that she knew she had never let him go. She hadn't walked away at all. Monica was right. She may have buried her love for Thomas, but it was alive and well. A tiny glowing ember in the dark. And she'd driven him away.

Monica saw Carla's face beginning to crumple and rushed over to her just in time. Pride reduced, Carla put her arms around the older woman's neck and wept, not caring who might come upon them in the basement as she did so.

Fifteen

Ezekiel sat outside Betty Jean's office building, where he'd been parked for the past fifteen minutes. He needed to talk to Betty Jean, but after the way she acted the last time, he was reluctant to go to the house. He figured no matter how much she might want Ezekiel sat outside Betty Jean's office building, where he'd been parked for the past fifteen minutes. He needed Ezekiel Ezekiel sat outside Betty Jean's office, where he'd been parked for the past fifteen minutes. He needed to talk to Betty Jean, but after the way she acted the last time, he was reluctant to go to the house. He figured no matter how much she migh want to, she wouldn't start acting a fool at her job. He still couldn't associate the naked screaming banshee throwing rocks from the front porch with his sweet Betty Jean, but then he couldn't associate his sweet Betty Jean with the woman who slept with a stranger the minute his back was turned, either.

Her betrayal hurt him, but he'd done a lot of thinking over the past few days and realized he missed her. He wanted to work things out with Betty Jean, so they could move on with the life they planned. He thought of Carla and felt a small stab of unease. He cared about Carla, but she'd changed. The Carla that mesmerized him for nearly a year hid herself from him now. They lived under the same roof, but he felt further away from her than when he only saw her in stolen glimpses. He didn't know if the strain in their relationship was caused by — no, he shook his head at the term. It wasn't a strain so much that affected them as it was a hollow space. Carla had become a hollow space. He'd talk to her or look over at her and she wouldn't be there. Her body was pressed up against his or just inches away, but Carla was gone. He didn't know if her absence was due to the loss of their child or because she no longer felt the same way about him.

He didn't know what caused the change in Carla, but as she withdrew further from him he began to feel more insecure. Carla's lack of interest was making him doubt himself and he didn't like it. He wanted Betty Jean back, he thought, resting his head against the car seat. Each time he was faced with Carla's cold indifference, it was plain she didn't care if he stayed or went, he thought of Betty Jean's warmth. He'd think of the way Betty Jean loved him and took care of him and he wanted to go home.

Home to *someone who loved him.*

And there stood his problem. He'd been sitting in his car all this time, he hadn't even removed his seat belt, because he didn't know if Betty Jean still loved him. He was afraid of going into the building and talking to her. He was terrified with a fear that had him gripping the steering wheel until his knuckles stood out prominently. Ezekiel noticed what he was doing and relaxed his grip on the wheel. He rested his head against his hands. He needed Betty Jean to love him again. He would do right this time. This would be the last chance she'd ever have to give him.

He was decided. He would have a talk with Betty Jean and Carla, both. He didn't want Betty Jean to think he was running from pillar to post and back again, so he would leave Carla's apartment, but not move straight back home. He'd get a room for a few nights, so Betty Jean would see he'd had some time alone to think. Then they could make up. Start fresh. He would move back home and they could put all this behind them. Soon, they'd be off to California together to enjoy a new life. Ready to execute his plan, he turned the key in the ignition and reversed the car from the parking lot.

**

Carla called to tell him she didn't need a ride home from work. She'd been acting so funny with him, especially since the last time he'd been to Betty Jean's; he was secretly happy for the excuse not to pick her up. He didn't know how she planned to get home and didn't ask. Besides, not having to pick her up gave him an opportunity to check into a hotel room. He stayed there practicing what he wanted to say and how to say it, until he was certain Carla was home.

He was going to tell her how he felt about her and how she was pushing him away from her. How he didn't want to go, but felt he had no choice. He wanted to word everything just right, so she'd know he cared for her. He didn't see any point in mentioning his eventual return to Betty Jean, so he wouldn't bring it up. No point in hurting her. He'd just tell the truth. He was leaving her apartment and getting a room, so he could work through his feelings. She told him her daughter was coming home that weekend and he could use that as an excuse, too, he thought.

He could say he didn't feel comfortable living with her with her little girl around. He could lay it on about morals and look like a good guy. After a few days he could call Carla and tell her it would be best if they ended it. No harm. No foul. No one's feelings got hurt. Ezekiel pulled into his usual parking space and got out of the car. This was not like when he'd gone to Betty Jean's office without a clue of what to say or do. This time he had a plan. So fear of the unknown did not paralyze him as he bounded up the stairs, two at a time, to knock at the door.

"It's open," Carla called from her chair in the living room. The lights were off, but the room was lit by the glow from the television set.

"Hey." His voice was lowered in respect of the quiet. She had the television on, but the sound was muted. He never could understand why she always did that. It irritated the hell out of him, too. Either she wanted to watch television or she didn't. He couldn't stand it when people couldn't make up their mind. He shut the door behind him, but stood just inside the room. He could hear music playing low in the bedroom. He knew it was something soft and bluesy even though he couldn't make out the lyrics.

"Hey, Zeke," she returned his greeting, a nervous smile on her lips.

"We need to talk." He started his prepared speech, then stopped, hesitating. She was looking all soft like the old Carla. Her mood was relaxed. He looked around but saw nothing burning in the ashtray. She hadn't been smoking. He frowned, curious about the change. If she wasn't high, then what?

"Yeah, I was thinking the same thing," Carla said slowly. She'd been home for over an hour and had plenty of time to think, but unlike Ezekiel, she hadn't rehearsed a speech. She was tired of talking and thinking. She'd only acted and done what she needed to do.

"I've been thinking maybe I should move out," he began just as he'd practiced. He paused to let what he was saying sink in and take effect, before he told her how he felt about her. He didn't want her to confuse what he was saying or think she could change his mind. He did care for her, but he was still moving out. Still going home.

"Yeah," Carla said in the same slow drawl she'd used before. "I've been thinking the same thing."

"Carla, I —" he was preparing to move forward with his speech, but stopped, not certain he'd heard her correctly. "What?"

"I've been thinking the same thing," she repeated casually. "You should move out. You're still caught up with your girl and I have enough drama of my own without buying tickets to someone else's play. I —" she stopped. She was about to say how she had issues of her own to work out regarding Thomas, but didn't, no longer wanting to discuss Thom with him at all. She changed directions, saying instead, "Well, the reasons

"I've been thinking the same thindon't really matter
"I've been thinking the same thing," she repeated casually. "You should move out. You're still caught up with your girl and I have enough drama of my own without buying tickets to someone else's play. I —" she stopped. She was about to say how she had issues of her own to work out regarding Thomas, but didn't, no longer wanting to discuss Thom with him at all. She changed directions, saying instead, "Well, the reasons don't really matter and as I've never been one for long, drawn-out good-byes —"

"Good-byes?" Though she'd been the one to broach the subject, he still couldn't admit the truth that he was leaving and breaking up with her. He raised an eyebrow, feigning a surprised look. "Why are you talking about good-bye? You think I want Betty Jean back, don't you? Why would you think I —"

Carla held up her hand, shaking her head. She closed her eyes, saying, "Don't Zeke. Don't shit me, okay? Just let it go. Don't try to turn me into an ass."

Silence held the room captive for a long time, then Carla used her chin to direct Ezekiel's attention behind him. In the time since she'd been home from work, she'd gone through the apartment gathering Ezekiel's things. She hadn't had the time nor the inclination to rehearse speeches. She'd merely done what needed to be done, like she always did. She handled her business. His things were stacked neatly in the corner behind the front door, waiting on him to gather them and go.

Ezekiel stared at his belongings, speechless. Carla was throwing him out of her apartment. He looked from his things piled by the door to Carla's impassive features. She'd better hope this wasn't a ploy to get his attention, he thought, as he stooped to collect his bags. If she was serious enough to pack his things, he was serious enough to actually leave. Without another word, he did.

Carla remained seated. Even after he'd pulled the door closed behind him, she sat unmoved. It was not until she heard his car pull away that she got up to lock and chain her front door.

**

Betty Jean greeted Wednesday morning feeling broken.

She was tired. Dog tired. It was the last Wednesday she'd be in her house, she thought heavily. Thursday would be the last day at an office where she'd spent the better part of seven years building her career. Her things were packed. The moving company, TransAtlantic, Inc., had been called. Everything was scheduled.

Their truck would be at her home the first thing Friday morning, before moving on to retrieve the meager possessions Sheila was bringing with her. Betty Jean planned to drive her Infiniti to California and would be pulling out with Sheila before the sun came up on Saturday. Everything was planned down to the very last detail.

Everything except Ezekiel.

She still didn't know what to do about their relationship. Part of her wanted him to come home, so they could work things out, and another part of her wanted him to come home, so she could tell him to kiss her ass. She'd put up with his shit for six years and counting, though. It was difficult to think about walking away and throwing up her hands when she had so much time invested in their relationship. Years that she couldn't get back and couldn't give to anyone else. Not that she would want to, she thought, shrinking away from the suggestion of being in a relationship with another man. Not when she couldn't deny that she still loved Ezekiel Johnson. Even with all his faults, she believed he could settle down if he wanted. He just wasn't ready yet, but in a year or two, who knew? If she walked away now, so close to the finish line.... She'd be giving a good man to some other woman. A man who got all his running around out in his youth and was prepared for the commitment of marriage. In a few years, she told herself, he'd be ready to settle down and it would be too late for her, because she gave up too soon.

She sighed heavily, sinking deeper into her pillow. Zeke was a good man, but that didn't stop him from continuously hurting her. It didn't stop him from trying to spread himself all over the place. *How much more could she take from him?* she asked herself. *Could she hold on until he sowed all his wild oats? Should she call him; talk to him? Forgive him? Give him another chance to screw you over,* her heart added. She was bombarded with questions and she rolled over, covering her head with her pillow, but her mind continued to pound out inquiries.

She was trapped beneath the weight of her problems. Which was why at 8:30 in the morning on one of her final days at work, instead of tying up loose ends in her business life, her personal life had her lying in bed. Crushed into the pillows. Broken.

Betty Jean looked around the room seeing Ezekiel's things peppered around the debris of her half packed bedroom and chewed at her bottom lip. *This will not do.* In forty-eight hours the movers would be there and she still didn't know if his things should be loaded on the truck with hers or left behind. She hadn't told him that they needed her in California earlier than scheduled, she thought judiciously, but he hadn't been quite fair with her, either. He came to their home and fucked her like she was nothing. Then tried to just leave.

Thinking on it made her angry again.

He'd been the one to do wrong for six years, but she was the one lying in bed pathetically feeling sorry for herself. *Well, no more*, she thought, rising from the bed. She was tired of feeling like a victim. Tired of allowing Ezekiel to make her feel like a fool and most recently, act like one. He only controlled her life because she turned the reins of it over to him a long time ago. What she needed to do was snatch them back. Instead, she was lying in bed waiting for him to return, just as she'd spent the last few years waiting for him to settle down and do right by her.

Why should she wait? she asked, pumping herself up for action. *Why shouldn't she pick up the phone and tell him she's had enough of this simple-minded ass game and for him to bring himself home pronto?* She'd been patient long enough, dammit. Ezekiel was going to make a decision one way or another and quit sitting on the fence. If he couldn't get his shit together, she'd help him! For once, she was going to take the bull by the horns and tell Mr. Johnson what was what.

With firm resolve Betty Jean sat up in bed reaching for the phone.

**

Friday evening Betty Jean stood in the center of her empty living room. The movers had left a few hours earlier and should be just about finished with Sheila's apartment. The few things she was adding onto the truck shouldn't take that long to load. True to her word, Sheila was only taking the essentials. She'd either sold, given away or thrown out most of her belongings. She would be staying with Betty Jean until she found something of her own and planned to purchase new furniture when she had a place to put it.

Betty Jean walked into the dining room of her old home. Smiling, she traced the pattern on the wallpaper with her finger. She remembered the weekend that she and Ezekiel hung it. They'd been in the house together for a few months working their way around it. They did most of the improvements and repairs themselves. After hanging the paper, they'd ordered pizza and sat on the floor in the newly covered dining room to eat it.

Ezekiel lit some candles and their light glowed beautifully off the walls. Betty Jean recalled the way his eyes looked with the candle's flame reflected in them and she touched her fingers to her lips in remembrance. His kiss had been so sweet.

Betty Jean visited each room of the house they'd shared. Warm memories greeted her from every corner. *They'd had their problems, but what couple didn't?* Love had filled their house and made it a home. Eventually, she found herself back in the front hall of the house. Since all the furniture and boxes were gone, she sat on the stairs, thinking.

She wanted California to be a fresh start. She wanted to leave all the hurt and pain here in the south. There would only be love and happiness in the golden state and she intended to bask in the glow. She wanted to be happy. The way she was before Ezekiel's infidelities started chipping away at her light.

Before all the others.

Before Carla.

Betty Jean took a calming breath, inhaling deeply. Carla would not be in California, she reminded herself.

She rubbed her clammy palms down her jeans, then glanced at her watch. Ezekiel called last night and she asked him to come to the house this evening. He'd agreed, saying he needed to talk to her as well, but she'd thought he'd be here by now. She remembered the last time she'd waited for him. He said 6:00 but showed up three hours late. She hoped she wasn't in for a repeat performance. She was waiting for Sheila to call and didn't want to leave her hanging if she was ready before Ezekiel arrived.

Maybe Carla wouldn't let him come, she thought, then shook her head against the possibility. Ezekiel was a grown man. He did what he wanted to do. If she, Betty Jean, couldn't dictate his actions and he was in love with her, then Carla sure as hell couldn't control what he did.

**

Ezekiel pulled into the driveway of his house. He turned off his headlights, but didn't exit the vehicle. Over the past few days, he'd done a lot of thinking in his little hotel room and the truth was he loved Betty Jean. After speaking to her on the phone, he'd asked himself over and over again if he could give up other women for her and he found that he could. He panicked a little at first and thought, no. But then he started thinking about Betty Jean and how she loved him like no one else and the notion of just the two of them started sounding better and better.

He knew that she didn't say she loved him anymore because of the other women. She told him once that she couldn't stop herself from loving him, but she wouldn't be fool enough to tell him how she felt anymore. He missed the sound of the words coming from her lips. He also knew what he had going on outside of their bedroom was the cause for her limitations within it. He could do anything he wanted to Betty Jean's body and she'd enjoy it, but wouldn't return any favors. She said whenever she caressed his body she started thinking about other women doing the same thing to him and it killed her mood.

Unconsciously, he grabbed himself. He couldn't remember the last time she'd put her lips around him. She had this thing she would do with her tongue...He shook his head to dislodge the image. He didn't want to walk into the house with a woody sticking out of his pants. She would think that's all he ever had on his mind and for once, she would be wrong. He didn't want just the piece of her that she hadn't closed off from him. He wanted her to open herself up to him completely again. He reached across to the glove compartment and withdrew a small velvet box.

He opened it and stared at the two carat diamond marquis ring he'd selected. Betty Jean had nothing else to worry about. He was through playing all the games that nearly caused him to lose her. They were going to go to California and live happily ever after. He snapped the lid closed on the box and stuffed it into his pocket as he climbed from the car.

**

The knock at the door made Betty Jean jump. Damn, she was tense. She rose from the steps, shaking her hands out in front of her. *Relax, relax, relax,* she closed her eyes, chanting softly.

She opened the door with a question. "Why are you knocking?" It was the first thing that came to mind. She winced, inwardly wishing she'd thought of something less aggressive to say. She was nervous, she told herself, accepting the excuse.

Ezekiel smiled, blushing. He was just as nervous as she was. "Hell, I didn't think to use my key. I'm nervous, I guess. I feel like I'm coming to pick you up for our first date." Ezekiel stepped into the empty hall, looking around in surprise. *Where was everything?* He started to ask, then thought that it could wait.

Betty Jean turned, leaning her back against the front door. "Were you nervous on our first date, Ezekiel?" It was hard to imagine him apprehensive. He was always confident and sure of himself. He had this sensual power that pulled her to him and she was sure other women felt the tug of it, too. Hell, over the years he proved they did.

She doubted he ever had cause to feel nervous about anything, least of all her and said so, before she could stop herself. She didn't want to sound confrontational tonight, it was the last thing she wanted. He didn't get angry, though. Her words only caused a brief sadness to cross his face when he looked up at her, but it was gone in an instant.

"Yeah, you made me nervous, BJ. I knew that with you I'd have to come correct, that you weren't going to put up with my bullshit." He smiled, recalling when they first met and his first impressions of her.

Betty Jean's eyes held his. "But I did, didn't I? Every last bit of it. I put your bullshit on toast and ate it like it was jelly, Zeke. Smiling, enjoying the taste, even if it killed me." She hadn't intended to sound so antagonistic, so angry, but the problem with holding something in for too long was that you couldn't always control it when it was ready to come out. Swallow your feelings enough and calm and easy becomes a well-shaken Coke, bubbling and ready to burst. She'd kept her silence long enough. She wanted to lay all the cards on the table. No hidden hurts would come along out west to stab her later.

He had the grace to bow his head. "I'm sorry for everything I've done, Betty Jean." He held out his hand to her. Leading her over to the staircase, they both sat down. Again, he wondered where all the furniture was and why she was staying in an empty house, but he shoved the questions aside. There would be time for them later. His things weren't in a fucking pile by the front door like at Carla's and he counted that as a good sign. He just wanted to get everything straight with Betty Jean.

"I've been doing a lot of thinking lately, BJ, about what I want. We've been through some rough times together and I know most of it was my fault. Even when it was you who started an argument or a fight, it was me at the root of it. I was the one messing everything up and giving you something to complain and fuss about. I wasn't doing right, Betty Jean."

"Why are you going through all this? It's history. It's done. We can't do anything but concentrate on the future now." Her voice was harsher than she would have liked, but she made no excuses for it. It seemed her emotions were going to let themselves be known, whether she tried to play nice or not. She didn't want to rehash old shit. No one knew better than she did what *they'd* been through together, even though she couldn't recall any sleepless nights he'd experienced. She wanted to focus on what was in front of them. The future.

He captured one of her hands from her lap and held it within his own for a long quiet moment. He'd messed up so many times with this woman. He thought about all the things he'd done behind her back. Some things made it to the light and she knew about them, but most remained in the dark, concealed from her, and he prayed they would always remain that way. He didn't want to lose Betty Jean. He really had done a lot of thinking since leaving Carla's apartment, and he didn't want to play anymore. Betty Jean was enough to satisfy him and he no longer needed the chase. He only needed to convince her he was telling the truth.

"I know you probably think I'm staying at some woman's house, but I'm at a motel."

"Some woman? If we must discuss this can we at least be real, Ezekiel? It never crossed my mind that you were at *some woman's* house. I would have placed my check on a bet that you were shacked up at Carla's house."

When Betty Jean finished speaking, Ezekiel felt the air leave his lungs in a great whoosh of retreat, but he held his tongue, hoping he looked calm on the outside. *How in the shit did she know about Carla?* he thought frantically. *How long had she known? What did she know?*

"I've been knowing about Carla since that last vacation you took from work. You got sloppy the last few days and left clues, but you always leave a trail, Zeke. Always. I used to think you did it on purpose, that you liked being caught," she said, answering the question he hadn't spoken aloud. The one she read in his face.

"When you would turn away from me sometimes at night, I would know it was because of her. I knew when you would get dressed to leave the house what you had planned for the evening just by which cologne you chose to wear. I know a lot of things about you, Ezekiel."

Squeezing her hand, he found his voice. Pleading, he said, "BJ, that's all behind me. If you want me to confess to all my sins, I will. I don't care. I'll do whatever I have to do to keep you with me. I played a lot of bullshit ass games over the years, but like you said, all that's history. I don't want anybody but you."

"Did you love Carla, Ezekiel?" She'd wondered about it for months and asked while she had the opportunity. If they were going for complete honesty, she might as well ask the hard stuff first.

"No." His answer was immediate and definite, echoing his bruised ego. "I love you, Betty Jean. She was just something stupid and physical that didn't mean anything to me."

"You would lose me over something stupid and meaningless." She had not asked a question. "You spent a lot of time with her, Ezekiel. That wasn't just about sex. You spent time with her even when you weren't having sex," she said, thinking about the movie tickets she'd found. "I thought we were being honest."

"Betty Jean, I'm being as honest with you as I know how to be. I love you, baby, I don't know what else to say." He raised his other hand, as if to touch her, but changed his mind. "I can't take back any of the shit I put you through. Whatever Carla was or wasn't to me, all she managed to be in the end was the person that opened my eyes. Carla made me see that I was a fool and I was going to mess around and lose you." He looked into her eyes, willing her to believe him. All he needed was this one last chance.

"I've been doing a lot of thinking myself, Ezekiel. We've been doing this a long time. Six years. We have to get to a place where we either move up to the next level or we call it quits, because we can't go any further."

Ezekiel reached into his pocket. His fingers closed around the ring box. *It's now or never*, he thought. He decided to just dive in and cut her off, saying, "I'm ready for the next step, Betty Jean. I —" *Why was she shaking her head?* He was getting a sick feeling in his stomach.

"I can't go any further," her words cut into his sentence. She slid her hand away from his and stood. She turned back to face him, repeating again, "I can't go any further, Ezekiel. I woke up a few days ago feeling so beaten. I was so weak I didn't even want to get out of bed. I picked up the phone, planning to call you and force you to come back to me. Ready to beg and plead while pretending that I was laying down the law."

"I'm here now, baby, and you didn't have to force me or pretend or do anything," he pleaded.

She spoke as though he hadn't. "I started dialing your number, but I hung up. I was lying there thinking that I keep making the same mistake. I keep forgiving you. I keep turning my head the other way hoping that you'll change. For six years now, I've been waiting patiently for the new Ezekiel to emerge."

"That's what I'm trying to tell you. I have changed. Loving me and giving me another chance isn't a mistake this time."

"It never was. The mistake wasn't in loving you, it was in hoping you would change. No one changed, except me. I slept with a man I didn't even know. In part, because of how bad I'd been feeling because of you. There was a little revenge in my actions, too. I gave some other man my body because it would hurt you. Even if you never found out, I wouldn't feel so bad when you were out with Carla. When you looked in my eyes to lie to me, there would have been a little lie of my own in them, but you wouldn't have seen it. You would have looked at me and only seen a fool. I'm running outside, naked, making a scene. It's just too much!" Again, she was taken back by the amount of anger that seized her.

Ezekiel stood slowly. *How had their conversation gotten so out of hand?* When he made to touch her, she recoiled. "Everything up to this very moment is behind us. It's in the past. I'm telling you I want to start over and get our life back."

Betty Jean looked at him silently with her lips pressed together. *Lord, how she loved this man, but he made her so weak.* Every time he hurt her the pain increased. Just thinking of the next mistruth made her knees feel like jelly. She'd open the mail some day and there would be a woman suing him for child support or they'd be receiving terminal news from the free clinic. They'd been lucky so far and nothing like that had happened. No babies. No diseases. But what happened when their luck ran out and it was time to pay the piper? Nothing done in the dark had ever been inclined to stay there. It wouldn't necessarily have to be a baby or a disease, either, that came to destroy them later. His being with another woman was traumatic in itself and she didn't want to risk the heartache again. She couldn't give any more of her life to Ezekiel.

She didn't think he could change. He'd try, but he'd revert to his old ways. He always did and she'd be crying and feeling low, like she always did. She reached into her pocket, withdrawing a small key ring that held two keys. She lifted Ezekiel's hand and placed the keys there.

"I'm telling *you*, I can't. I can't do this anymore, Ezekiel." Betty Jean's cell phone rang and she picked it up, okaying into the receiver. "I'll be there in a second." She retrieved her purse from where it hung on the front door-knob and dug out her car keys. Opening the front door, she said, "I put your things in that storage place about two blocks up from here on South Durbin. You know the place."

He nodded in a daze. He was still looking down at the keys in his hand. His brain refused to process the information it was receiving. *Why were his things in storage?* Betty Jean stepped out on the porch, looking back at him, but there was nothing left to be said. Again, she turned to go. She'd crossed her front lawn for the last time and was opening her car door when Ezekiel came out onto the porch.

"You're just going to leave? Just like that? After all we've been through together? After all these years?" He was angry. He'd lost for the second time in a matter of days. Twice now, his shit had been packed for him. "You think you're proving something, Betty Jean? Is that what this is supposed to be about? You're trying to prove you can be happy without me? That you don't need me? That your new job and moving to California will be enough to replace me? Enough to satisfy you when you come home and I'm not there? An empty echoing house is what you want?"

Betty Jean curled her lip in contempt. "Don't come to me with all that *after all these years* bullshit. You didn't give a fuck about all our years together when you were creeping out and creeping *in* to Carla. You weren't worried about me and what I wanted then." She got into her car, slamming the door behind her. She rolled her window down, saying, "Secondly, I'm pretty damned satisfied right now. I feel lighter and freer than I have in years. When I go home at night you're right, I won't have you there waiting for me, but I'll have peace of mind. And that's a pretty fair trade off if you ask me."

She let the window rise, sealing her away from Ezekiel before he could speak again. She'd been listening to him for too long as it was. She pushed the play button on her CD player, and turning up the volume, she let the song fill the car. She backed out from the driveway, singing:

The time is right, I'm gonna pack my bags
and take that journey down the road
'cause over the mountain I see the bright sunshine
and I want to live inside the glow

She stopped at the corner of her street, thinking it would be the last time she sat at that intersection. She looked around smiling. She'd told Ezekiel the truth, she did feel lighter. She felt good. Her car was packed and she was heading for *the bright sunshine.* All her worries and concerns about her future were gone. California was going to be a good thing for her, she thought picking up the song again:

I wanna go to a place where I can hold the intangible
and let go of the pain with all my might
I wanna go to a place where I'm suspended in ecstasy
somewhere between dark and light, where wrong becomes right

It was time to go. With a final look around, Betty Jean signaled for a turn. A moment later, she was gone.

Sneak Preview of the next Betty Jean title

Getting up and Getting on

Coming Soon

check website at www.mbridges05.com for details

Chapter One

She could see the twinkling lights of the city below her. Content, she sighed, sipping at her wine. Resting her head against the cushion on her lounge chair, she sung along with the music streaming out from the living room through the patio door she'd left open.

There will be mountains that I will have to climb
And there will be battles that I will have to fight
Victory or defeat, it's up to me to decide
But how can I expect to win, if I never tried

"*I just can't give up now —*" she started on the chorus before realizing that she sung alone. The vocals of Mary, Mary no longer accompanied her. Confused by the interruption, she turned in her chair to see Sheila strolling through the patio doors.

"I only paused it, don't worry. Whatcha got up for tonight other than the usual, *I'm just going to enjoy some peace and solitude* crap?"

In response, Betty Jean rolled her eyes before turning back to her view of the city. "I'm perfectly content to —"

"Just sit here." Sheila said the last few words in unison, having heard them for the past several months. She poured wine into the glass she'd brought with her from the kitchen. With a sip from her glass, she took a seat across from Betty Jean.

Neither woman spoke for a moment. Sheila sat staring into her glass searching for the words she wanted to say. They'd been in California for nearly eight months and aside from a handful of times when they first arrived, Betty Jean refused to go out with her. It wasn't that Sheila was a party horse, she wasn't. She just didn't like the way Betty Jean was burying herself. As far as Sheila knew, Betty Jean hadn't dated since their move and *Sheila knew.*

"Come with me to the Chicken Shack," she said, abruptly breaking into both their thoughts.

"I don't know. I don't feel like booty shaking tonight," Betty Jean said, frowning at the thought of going to a club. She didn't feel like shouting to be heard, being bumped into, ground against, leered at or lied to and she couldn't seem to get her friend to understand. She really was content just sitting at home.

"Is that the only excuse, I mean reason, you have for not wanting to come with me?" Sheila raised a brow, asking the question into her glass before sipping again.

"Yeah, I guess." Betty Jean's reply was wary. Why did she get the feeling she was walking into a trap? She got a vivid image of the last time she went out at Sheila's urging and she shook her head, trying to back away from any potential snares. "I'm just not feeling the noise of a nightclub."

"So, no dancing and music?"

"No."

"Okay, cool." Sheila grinned and her eyes lit up with mischief. "The Chicken Shack is a poetry house. Kinda

Love Jones-type ambiance. Since the loud music and dancing are your only objections, you have no reason not to go. It's going to be fun." Sheila stood, draining her glass.

"Come on, Sheila," Betty Jean groaned, closing her eyes.

Sheila stared down at Betty Jean, shaking her head. "I love you, Betty Jean. You're one of the best people I know, so I have to tell you this," she paused, uncharacteristically hesitating to say what was on her mind. Regaining her seat, she reached for Betty Jean's hand. "You can't stop living. Now before you go shaking your head, let me talk. You aren't living, baby, you're existing. You go to work, you come home. That's it. You wouldn't give anybody the time of day if you were wearing two watches. How long are you going to mourn, Betty Jean?"

"Mourn?" Angry, Betty Jean snatched her hand away. "Stop talking crazy. What the hell am I mourning?" She rose, pulling her robe closed. She padded angrily across the deck, going towards the house, on the pretense of getting ice.

Sighing, Sheila rose to follow her.

Betty Jean wasn't getting away from her so easily. Now that the subject had been broached, she was going to see it through. *In for a penny, in for a pound,* she thought before saying, "Mourning for yourself. The loss of Ezekiel and what could have been. Hell I don't know, Sweetie. I only know it's barely 7:30 in the evening on a Friday and you're wearing your bathrobe. Unless you're going to work, you're always in that damned thing and to tell you the truth, I half expect you to show up in it at Hurstwode and Donovan one day!"

Pulling the freezer door open with more force than was required, Betty Jean reached for an ice tray. "Damnit, Sheila, what's so spectacularly wrong with me wanting some peace and quiet?"

"Having peace and quiet and pulling the covers up over your head aren't the same thing. Which one are you doing? There's just no way in hell you're going to convince me that this is what you want. Your bathrobe on a Friday night. *Every Friday night.*"

"Well, it is." Betty Jean turned to face her friend. "All I have right now is peace and quiet and it's all I want. No bullshit. No drama. No headaches —"

"No life. No Zeke," Sheila cut in. She pretended not to see Betty Jean flinch. "Why are you letting him win?"

Frowning deeply, Betty Jean said in a low voice, "I'm not."

"Yes, you are," Sheila said, pushing through her guilt. The two of them had grown close and the last thing she wanted was to hurt Betty Jean. But watching her zombie her way through life was hurting. She couldn't sit back quietly and let it happen anymore.

Betty Jean's trembling fingers couldn't remove the cubes from the tray, so she slammed it upside down on the counter. The sugar bowl rattled and she stopped, staring at it. She dropped her head, closing her eyes for a brief moment. "I haven't let him win anything." She tucked a long strand of hair behind her ear. The action echoed her vulnerability, but Sheila plunged on.

"Okay, fine. Call him." Sheila removed the cordless phone from its cradle, extending it towards Betty Jean. "Call him. See if he's sitting at home lost, confused, barricaded against life. I'm your only companion, Betty Jean, and I'm scared of moving out and leaving you alone. This time next month I'll be in my own place, then what? You can't stop living 'cause I guarantee you, he hasn't. Hurt feelings and all, believe me, he's rolling on. Don't be afraid of being hurt again. Hell, be afraid of hurting somebody else this time around! Let somebody else shake and tremble at the mention of Betty Jean's name.

"Sweetie, you had the courage and strength to leave Zeke. Now I'm just saying it's time to get up and get on with it. You have a new life. A fresh beginning. Stop sitting at the start line and join the damned race." Placing the phone on the counter, she touched Betty Jean lightly on the shoulder. "It's fine to listen to your gospel music trying to let it heal you, but hear what it's saying. There's a message in it. You have to try, Betty Jean and sitting here locked in your safe, lovely house, away from the world and the living is not trying. It's giving up." She left the kitchen for her room, pausing to restart the CD Betty Jean had been listening to and Mary, Mary filled the room again.

"There's a new poet doing a reading and signing autographs. I forget her name, but her book is *Too Deep for Tears*. It's a collection of poetry and short stories. Hell, with the title alone, I'm interested. I'm getting dressed and going to check it out. You're welcome to come along." Her voice faded as she turned a corner and Betty Jean stared down at the phone.

She still knew his office number by heart. His cell phone number was a little sketchy, but she knew with a little thought and concentration it would come to her, as well. She thought of Sasha and shuddered. He'd rot in hell before she called his cell phone. The last time she dialed that number she got a whole earful of something she didn't want to hear.

Music suddenly blasted from the back of the house roaring from Sheila's bedroom and Betty Jean jumped at the unexpected noise. Rap music screamed from the Kenwood speakers and she recalled Sasha screaming Zeke's name. The woman rapping was telling some man to kiss her ass and Betty Jean found herself concurring with the sentiment, Ezekiel Johnson could rot in hell just the same, even without her calling his cell phone! Sweeping the ice tray into the sink, melting ice and all, she left the kitchen. Racing to her own bedroom, she hurried through a shower, mentally searching her wardrobe for something to wear.

**

Sheila was right, Betty Jean thought, the poetry house did have a Love Jones ambiance. It was dimly lit with small domed candles on each table. Only the small circular stage offered any real light and even that was shadowed. They'd heard two poets already and were waiting for the evening's star attraction to come out on stage.

"How about another round?" Sheila asked, looking around for the waitress.

"I've had my eye out for the waitress for the last few minutes, but it's such a crush in here I don't spot her until she's fading back into the crowd again. I keep getting pulled into the performances. She'll slip my mind until it's too late to catch her attention." Betty Jean looked around smiling, glad she'd come out for the night.

"Speaking of having an eye out, that guy over there —" Sheila leaned in towards Betty Jean about to point, but was interrupted by the poet who'd come onto the stage.

The woman stood for a moment, until the house was completely quiet. Then lowering her head, she perched on the edge of the stool that was placed in the middle of the stage.

"*Cravings.*" The voice sounded husky and seductive and the few patrons who had lowered their conversations, but not stopped talking, fell silent. In a hypnotic trance, all eyes turned towards the stage and the petite woman, lured by her voice.

"*I seek your arms around my waist.*" She breathed slowly into the microphone until her voice filled the room, replacing the air.

"*I crave your lips upon my face. I want your scent on my hair.*" The woman ran a hand slowly through her cropped curls, sucking in her breath sharply. She exhaled the next two lines in a rush of sensual sound. "*I need you here. I need you there.*

"*Temptation, that's this strong, in itself could not be wrong. Loving you all night long.*" The woman speaking smiled slowly, nodding her head in agreement to the luried suggestion. "*To you I should belong.*"

Her smile suddenly faded and she frowned, rising from the stool. Her voice was harder when she commanded, "*Don't shake your head to cause me grief,*" but there was a whisper of fear in her eyes. She wrapped her slender arms around her body, hugging herself. "*Just hold me tight and then release.*" She flung her arms wide with the word. "*Do all the things your heart feels. Touch my soul and make it real.*"

She sat again on the stool, first sagging in gratified contentment, then stretching long and straight on the stool. Her words came faster. "*Arch my back, make me cry, let me know that I'm alive. Love me till I think I'll die.*" The word echoed through the room and she paused, surveying the entranced audience before adding in a breathless whisper, "*Then sigh, content and satisfied. Look at me through lids half shut.*" Her own were half closed and heavy lidded.

"*I think I love you, but —*" She was shaking her head in the negative. Despair was written clearly in her expressive features and the audience waited, sharing her heartache. "*Arms so strong should bare my name, not just a minute's pleasure from a timeless game. Kiss me deeply, like the ones we stole.*" A sweet smile spread across her face, a strange mixture of strength and weakness. "*And once again lay claim to my soul.*"

There was a brief moment of stunned quiet as the crowd regained itself that was followed by thunderous applause. The poet smiled shyly, took a sip of water and launched into another piece. Fifteen minutes later, Betty Jean sat back in her booth with a hand to her chest. "She was incredible. I liked all the poetry this evening, but *that* was performance art. She has such wonderful control of her voice."

"I'm going to get an autograph later," Sheila said, absently searching the crowd for the man she'd seen earlier. All through the poet's set, his attention had been on Betty Jean. Now Sheila couldn't find him. A shame, too, because even from a distance, she could tell he was a hotty. Pushing him from her mind, she gave her attention back to Betty Jean. "So, what did you think? Worth getting out of your bathrobe for?"

"Worth getting out of my bathrobe for," Betty Jean conceded, laughing.

"Exactly, the reaction I was seeking," a male voice cut in from just behind Betty Jean's left ear and she stiffened, her eyes wide.

Sheila stared across the table at the man she'd seen in the crowd. Up close, as promised from far away, he was a handsome devil. There was something familiar about him, though; she was certain she'd never met him. A name might slip her mind, but damned if she'd forget a face like that, especially when it was attached to such a body.

"Amaretto Sour, I believe." With an exaggerated flourish he placed a glass before Betty Jean. "Courvoisier with a splash of Ruby Red grapefruit juice for the leggy one."

When Sheila lifted an eyebrow at his words, he held up his hands in mock defense. "Don't blame me, I'm only repeating what the waitress said. *Amaretto Sour for the Cutie in Blue and Courvoisier with a splash of Ruby Red for the leggy one.*"

"Why didn't you repeat the Cutie in Blue part when she got her drink?" Sheila playfully sucked on her straw, a breath away from flirting with the tall stranger.

"Because," he explained, seating himself beside Betty Jean in the booth, "I'm saving her for myself."

"And the lesbian waitress can have me, is that it?" Sheila asked laughing, reluctantly tapping down her attraction. He'd made his choice when he slid into the other side of the booth.

To this, the man merely hunched his shoulders, a grin stretching across his features. "I don't judge. Women are beautiful, sexy. I don't blame your kind." Sheila gave him a look and he laughed out loud, teasing. "Sorry, but I spotted Cutie in Blue first." He pulled his attention from Sheila back to Betty Jean's stunned face.

He doesn't remember me, she thought wildly. He'd hunted her down back home, sprouting all sorts of nonsense about connecting with her and wanting to get to know her better, but less than a year later and he didn't even recognize her.

Betty Jean took a long swallow of her drink, grateful the bartender had a generous hand with the alcohol and decided to go along with it. If Byron had forgotten her, so be it. If he wanted to pretend that they were strangers, she could, too. Hell, they were! It would be no real stretch of the imagination to act as though she didn't know him. She could forget him just as easily. No, great trick that would be, she mumbled into her glass, taking another long drink.

Sheila raised an eyebrow at Betty Jean's nearly empty glass. It was not like her friend to suck down a drink, but she tactfully refrained from making any comment. The table's newest arrival; however, had no such qualms.

"I don't usually drive women to drink until after we've dated," he joked. Having observed the two women since they first entered the club, he didn't think she was a lush. He smiled inwardly. This woman was having a really strange reaction to him. Either their chemistry didn't mix at all or he was missing a piece of the puzzle. His smile grew. He liked enigmas. And this one looked like it was wrapped up in a bit of mystery, too. Double the goodies.

Betty Jean didn't even try to keep the nastiness out of her voice. "I guess you just have that kind of effect on me."

"Want to be able to blame anything you may do on the alcohol, hun?" He winked at her, goading her further and she nearly kicked him under the table. The only thing that stilled her foot was that the move would be really awkward with him sitting beside her in the circular booth and she might strike Sheila by accident. Then she'd have to explain why she was playing footsy under the table.

"I'm grown. An adult," she said, completely contradicting her last thoughts that proved the contrary. Adults didn't kick people under the table. "I don't need an excuse to do anything. And if I were to do something, I wouldn't use alcohol for my reasoning. I'd want to be clear headed. That way, later I wouldn't have difficulty remembering anything I'd done," she snapped.

Eyebrows raised above the rim of her glass, Sheila tried to understand the hostility emanating from her friend. She knew Betty Jean was a little bit off men at the moment and she didn't blame her, but damn! It wasn't like her to attack like she was doing now. She usually just displayed cool disinterest and politely refused any offers to exchange numbers. Why she'd want to do that to the fine bit of goodness sitting next to her was beyond Sheila's realm of comprehension. It was all she could do to keep from eating him up with her eyes. He'd chosen the left side of the booth to sit his fineness in, not the right.

Betty Jean reached for her pocket book, belatedly thinking to pay for their drinks. She didn't want Byron's charity. He stopped her with a wave of his hand. "They're on the house."

"Why?" Betty Jean demanded. Her look, completely pugnacious. "Are we the one millionth customers at the Chicken Shack?;" she asked sarcastically. "No, thank you. I've learned how unwise it is to let a man buy me a drink in a strange night club."

He turned his head to stare at her and her stomach flipped a little recalling the touch of his lips on her thigh. A touch he obviously didn't remember. Suddenly, a smile came into his eyes and pulled at the corner of his mouth. He continued to stare at her, but there was a subtle difference in his gaze and she began to feel uneasy. Why was he looking like that, like he knew something she didn't? What was he thinking? Was he remembering something? She frowned. "Stop staring at me," she snapped, turning her head. Bastard.

He stared at her a moment longer before looking back at Sheila, who laughed as she sipped her drink. "Right about now you're wishing you went for the leggy one, hun?"

He should have, but he was a man of principle. He did like Leggs. She was sexy, tempting as sin. Wild, he could tell. There was a taunt in her eyes when she looked at him. A tease on her full lips, but as much as he liked a good taunt and a little tease, he'd spotted Cutie first.

Smiling, he slid from the booth, bidding them both good night.